Adam's Eden

Books by Faith Baldwin

Three Women
Departing Wings
Alimony
The Office Wife
The Incredible Year
Make-Believe
Today's Virtue
Skyscraper
Week-End Marriage
District Nurse
Self-Made Woman
Beauty
White-Collar Girl
Love's A Puzzle
Innocent Bystander
Wife Versus Secretary
Within A Year
Honor Bound
The Puritan Strain
The Moon's Our Home
Private Duty
The Girls of Divine Corners
Men Are Such Fools!
That Man Is Mine
The Heart Has Wings
Twenty-Four Hours A Day
Manhattan Nights
Enchanted Oasis
Rich Girl, Poor Girl
Hotel Hostess
The High Road
Career By Proxy
White Magic
Station Wagon Set
Rehearsal For Love
"Something Special"
Letty and the Law
Medical Center
And New Stars Burn
Temporary Address: Reno
The Heart Remembers
Blue Horizons
Breath of Life

Five Women in Three Novels
The Rest of My Life With You
Washington, U.S.A.
You Can't Escape
He Married a Doctor
Change of Heart
Arizona Star
A Job For Jenny
No Private Heaven
Woman on Her Way
Sleeping Beauty
Give Love the Air
Marry For Money
They Who Love
The Golden Shoestring
Look Out For Liza
The Whole Armor
The Juniper Tree
Face Toward the Spring
Three Faces of Love
Many Windows
Blaze of Sunlight
Testament of Trust
The West Wind
Harvest of Hope
The Lonely Man
Living By Faith
There Is A Season
Evening Star
The Velvet Hammer
Any Village
Take What You Want
American Family
No Bed of Roses
Time and the Hour
New Girl in Town
Thursday's Child
Adam's Eden

POETRY
Sign Posts
Widow's Walk

Adam's Eden

❧

Faith Baldwin

Holt, Rinehart and Winston / New York

Copyright © 1977 by Faith Baldwin Cuthrell

Published simultaneously in Canada by Holt, Rinehart and Winston of Canada, Limited.

Library of Congress Cataloging in Publication Data

Cuthrell, Faith Baldwin, 1893–
  Adam's Eden.

  I. Title.
PZ3.C973Ad [PS3505.U97]   813'.5'2   76-29898
ISBN 0-03-018896-2

First Edition

Designer: Kathy Peck
Printed in the United States of America

10 9 8 7 6 5 4 3 2 1

This story is naturally dedicated to my grandsons, who probably won't read it; but, in order not to make waves, also to my granddaughters, who probably will; and to Dorothy, who asked me, "What happened to Adam?"

To all,
with love

Adam's Eden

1

The village of Little Oxford has been for many years inordinately proud of its spring and autumn weather—which one assumes is now more clement that it was in the late 1600s when the village was founded. Every year since its weekly newspaper had first been published, there had been an editorial in May and October extolling these respective seasons. But this year Si Westcott, owner and publisher, had to find excuses; the shifting of the ice cap perhaps, the Gulf Stream, cloud seeding, distant earthquakes, pollution—he blamed everything but the Congress. For May was reluctant and willful—she blew hot and cold, rain fell in torrents, thunder crashed; lightning flickered, flashed, and sometimes bolted and struck. And in mid-May on a day that had turned sunny, though cool, Vanessa Steele was confronted by her personal Mayday.

When she suffered her moderate heart attack around four that afternoon, there had ensued a sort of disciplined confusion. Edna Collins, the young woman who, to Vanessa's grudging gratitude, looked after her, telephoned Vanessa's medical advisers—there were two, father and son. The elder Dr. Irvington summoned an ambulance and broke the speed limit getting to Vanessa's house. Edna also called Stacy Osborne, Vanessa's neighbor across the fields, and young Mrs. Osborne notified Vanessa's daughter-in-law in Westchester; her son was on a commuter train from the city. Stacy also called Vanessa's grandson, Adam Steele, who was spending the weekend with his current girl, also in Westchester. He always furnished his grandmother with a list of telephone numbers where he could be reached—"in case you break another arm," he explained.

Stacy went with Vanessa in the ambulance, saw her safely into Emergency and then into Intensive Care. But no one notified Vanessa's long-time companion, Shadow, the big black cat who, on the sight of the ambulance and stretcher, set his massive jaw and vanished.

Stacy got a lift home from a friend who was a volunteer at the hospital. From her big Victorian house, recently sold, Stacy telephoned her husband, Lee, at his office and when he heard the news he asked, "Anything I can do?"

"No. I'll notify people, but no one can see Van yet except her family. Edna and I will manage."

"Did you bring Shadow home with you? I think he'd be less unhappy, although he isn't hostile to Edna."

"Good Lord!" said his wife. "I forgot all about him. I'll get right over."

Vanessa hadn't spoken of Shadow; she'd been too

preoccupied with the oxygen. Besides, thought Stacy, overcome with guilt, she knew we'd take him.

When she arrived at the Steele house, as usual by the back door, Edna was on the back porch, her eyes reddened by tears.

"How is she?"

"In Intensive Care. Both Doctor Ben and his father are there. I've notified Vanessa's family. We can manage if they come and stay, but I doubt they will, except maybe Adam. Cora will help—I've no idea what I'd do without Cora. Of course she'll go with us when we move into Emily Warner's house, though it is so much smaller.... Where's Shadow?"

"I haven't seen him," said Edna, "since before Mrs. Steele was taken sick."

"Let's look."

They looked upstairs and down, in cellar and attic; they called; they walked over the fields and by stone walls. Edna went up the street to inquire at her own home and at neighbors'; Stacy walked around the corner to the Barker farm.

"He'd never come here," said Angie Barker earnestly. "He hates coming here. We still have old Jupiter, Dad's big dog."

"How is your father, Angie?"

"His disposition is terrible," Angie reported, "and I don't blame him, he's always been so active."

"He's lucky to have you," Stacy said, smiling. Angie Barker was a handsome girl; all the Barkers were handsome. Angie was a licensed practical nurse and lived at home with her parents and younger siblings. Ted,

3

the only boy now resident, was in trade school. The two older siblings were married and lived out of the area. Angie's younger sisters were in high school, a senior and a sophomore.

"I suppose so," Angie said, "but he doesn't think so. And he worries about the farm. But we all help. We've had to cut down of course, so it's now just vegetables—and Mom's flowers…. I do hope you find Shadow, Mrs. Osborne."

"If I don't, it will be catastrophic," Stacy said. "Mrs. Steele's in the hospital."

"What happened?"

Stacy told her; Angie looked troubled. She asked, as had everyone, "Is there anything I can do?"

"Perhaps when she gets home," Stacy answered, suddenly glad that while looking for Shadow she'd had time to talk with Angie. "I don't know when that will be or what treatment she'll require, but if it's a case of baths, injections, or whatever"—she shrugged—"perhaps you'll find the time to help? You know Mrs. Steele—she can't tolerate people she doesn't know."

"Or some she does."

"That's right, but she's always liked your family."

"She used to walk up here with Shadow. Sometimes, if we tied Jupiter up, she'd come in—and visit with Mom, or go out in the fields to talk to Dad."

"First time I ever saw her," Stacy said, "she came to the studio with Shadow, a basket of your vegetables, flowers, and a box of eggs. Scared me out of my shoes."

"She never scared me," Angie said. "She always talked

to kids as if they were her age. She came around when she heard of Dad's stroke. She said she couldn't send him flowers from his own farm, so she'd have someone take books to him in the hospital. He always liked detective stories. He reads a lot now and gets about with a walker and a wheel chair. He's a strong man," Angie said. "He says he'll lick this inconvenience yet, and Dr. Irvington says he wouldn't be surprised."

As Stacy turned away, Angie added, "Please give Mrs. Steele my love when you see her. Tell her I'll come by the hospital every so often and visit her when she comes home.... I hope you find Shadow," she said again.

Stacy and Lee found Shadow's body the next morning in a patch of wood beyond the stone wall, on their property. And Stacy asked, "How will we tell Van?"

"Call Bing Irvington," her husband advised. "I'll bury Shadow in Van's yard and mark the place."

When Stacy reached him, Dr. Irvington said, "Damn it!" He added, "She shows every indication of pulling out of this, but she's going to have to be more careful than she likes.... I'll tell her, Stacy. She's been expecting it, I think, not that Shadow might not have had a few more years, barring accident—a tough old cat," said Bing. "Do you know what happened?"

"No. He was just lying there as if he were asleep."

Vanessa knew. She wasn't told until she was out of the Intensive Care Unit and in her room. She had, of course, asked about Shadow at intervals, and Bing or his son had answered "He's been taken care of, Van."

But on the day before visitors—"No visitors until Tuesday," Bing had said—he told her. She was very quiet. Bing watched her carefully and at last she said, "Thanks. I knew it...I think. I also believe I know what happened. When he saw the ambulance and me on the stretcher, he decided I wasn't coming back this time, so he just went away by himself.... Thank Lee and Stacy for me."

"I'll let them come to see you soon and anyone else you wish, but not in clumps. You're not to get tired, Van."

"When my devoted, if stuffy, son tiptoed into Intensive Care while his wife sat outside, weeping as usual, I thought: How *could* you do this to me, Bing Irvington?"

"They're family; they had to be notified."

"Warren is determined to put me in one of those palatial rest homes, crawling with smiling nurses, doctors, and hundreds of old people, fortunate only in that they have money or that their children have, just sitting there—people in waiting. I told him I'd rather die and would do so immediately if he suggested it again. Adam, on the other hand, came in for the indicated three minutes and said, 'Time you got up, Gran, and raised a little hell.' He also told me I'd see him as soon as you'd let me go home."

"You will. He's rented the Osborne studio, now that Sara and Sam have moved out."

"You mean he'll commute to the city? I can't believe it."

"Oh, no. He's taking up residence in Little Oxford.

6

Until everything's settled, I'm not to tell you more than that. He said, 'Give her just enough to chew on. Curiosity will keep her alive, Bing. She won't die, before she figures things out, and I'll see to it that she doesn't.'"

"I just may, to spite him," Vanessa said.

"He loves you," Bing said gently. "He also hates the city and whatever business he's in."

"It's his father's," Vanessa said. "Adam stayed out of it as long as he could—college, Europe, and the alleged musical group he managed. He's inherited something of my gypsy blood.... He isn't in trouble, is he?"

"Only with his parents," said Bing. "I'm going now. Dr. Evans will be in to see you."

"I don't like him," said Vanessa. "I'm not yet senile. You and Ben, especially Ben," she added with the familiar gleam in her enormous eyes, "should know enough about hearts. I didn't need a specialist."

"Your son thought you did," said Bing, and he left the room, followed by a faint hoot of laughter. At the door he looked back. Vanessa, with her wild white hair, her lean brown face, looked quite as old as she was, but burned somehow with a stubborn indestructible spirit. She'd be after him again about her forbidden cigars. He remembered when she'd been in this hospital before and Lee Osborne had smuggled some in to her. No cigars now and, of course, no Shadow to go home to.

"She didn't cry," Bing told his wife later, and Letty Irvington said, "Of course not. I think she's cried, inside, for some years, knowing this was bound to happen. I'm sorrier for Shadow, really. If he'd been just a little

7

more psychic, he wouldn't have gone into the woods and committed suicide."

"Suicide? How fanciful can you get?" asked Bing.

"It's a form of suicide when you simply give up.... May I see her?"

"You and everyone else, if and when she'll have you, after she gets home. But Adam's coming here to live will be the best medicine anyone can prescribe."

"What will he live on?"

"Not his grandmother. He has his trust fund, you know, and when he's thirty, he'll come into the principal. His parents can't stop him from doing what he wants. Very dull good people," he added. "I wonder how they produced him?" Irvington said.

"I daresay in the conventional way," Letty answered, "which reminds me, have you decided when we can absent ourselves long enough to visit our daughter and her family?"

"I thought during July. In August Ben and Amy are thinking of that cruise—if we'll take Benjy."

"Of course we'll take Benjy, although when he was still in the cradle or even a playpen he was less hair-raising. But Ben said he couldn't afford the cruise."

"He can't, but he said that the way things are going he'll be less able to afford it next year. He and Amy have been talking for months about going for broke on a vacation. The reason they decided on the cruise was that there would be no planes to catch, no hotel reservations, no screaming phones, just sea and sun— they'll get a lot of the former, I dunno about the latter—

8

and only as much sightseeing as they want at every port."

"How's Stacy?"

"Fine—and, as usual, level-headed, which is astonishing in an artist. She's upset about Van and, of course, Shadow. Why do you ask?"

"I think she's pregnant."

"Why?"

Letty shrugged, and Bing looked at the lamplight shining on her silver-gilt hair. It was no more silver than gilt but as curly as it had been when she was eighteen, and he thought: I'm a fortunate man.

He said, "I should be accustomed to your flights of fancy, but she hasn't been to see me, or said anything to me, or, as far as I know, to our more popular son."

"He's not more popular, just younger, which isn't always an advantage."

"You haven't told me why yet."

"It's a sort of look," Letty answered.

"Okay.... If she comes to the office, I'll let you know and then send her to Joe Roberts."

Dr. Joseph Roberts was Chief of Obstetrics; Bing had given up the delivering of infants some years before and Ben had not officiated at births since he became his father's partner.

"When may Van come home?"

"That's up to Evans."

"I dread it for her," Letty said, her eyes filling.

Bing said hastily, "She has a backbone second to none and she's logical."

9

"Doesn't help," his wife said.

Bing shifted the subject to their vacation. They hadn't seen their daughter Cynthia for almost a year. They'd flown out briefly when Cynthia's third child, and first son, had been born and she'd told her father, "That's the last one. Bill was hankering for a boy and mother yearned for another Benjamin, but I'm damned if I'm going to assist in the overpopulation of a perfectly ghastly world."

"It's the only one we have at present, and so far what you've contributed to it has been pretty good. Couldn't you call him something else?" her father had asked. "Too many Benjamins confuse me."

"Not when this one will be living in California. Besides he's only the third or fourth or whatever it is, and his middle name is William. I intend to call him Willie."

Vanessa was to go home to a downstairs bedroom, once a catchall off the living room. It would be ample for her needs, and there was a downstairs lavatory. When she growled, in her baritone fashion, about baths, Dr. Evans suggested that she install a shower.

"I can't afford it," she told him, "and I hate showers."

Bing, who was present, asked, "How about Warren?"

"My son," she admitted, "would gladly build me a Roman bath.... I suppose it's guilt," she added obscurely, "although God knows *I* should feel it and not Warren. But I don't. I'm an adamantly sinful, selfish, unregenerated character," she added to the heart specialist's embarrassment. He'd never laid eyes on Vanessa

10

Steele before her illness. "And I intend to remain so," she ended. "Bing, tell me about Adam?"

"I told you...he's rented the studio."

"What is he going to do? Manage another combo and play in bars?"

"I've no idea."

"Why can't he live with me? There are two bedrooms upstairs. I can trust him with Edna."

Bing said, "I'm amazed that anyone dare live with you, Van, including Edna."

"We get along," Vanessa said, "and she's well paid."

Stacy brought Vanessa home in mid-June and, as they entered the house, Vanessa said abruptly, "Don't expect me to go out to see where Shadow is yet."

"Take your time," Stacy answered. "It's near the stone wall and marked."

"If there's a heaven for cats," said Vanessa, "I doubt he's there."

She shook going into the house, but there was Edna waiting, and the downstairs bedroom arrangement to inspect. After a while, Dr. Evans had said, she could go upstairs and down again once a day. Later, she could take reasonable exercise—walking, for instance. The bike was out, along with tobacco. However, a moderate amount of alcohol was indicated—if she was accustomed to it.

"Damn fool!" Vanessa had commented crossly to Ben. "I'll probably become an alcoholic. Edna can cook, but if there's anything that revolts me, it's good plain New England cooking."

11

"So teach her," suggested Ben. "You can sit in the kitchen rocker and reveal the mysteries of gourmet cuisine. It will be helpful to her, especially when she marries."

"Not if she marries that young oaf she sees on her days off."

The downstairs bedroom faced southwest and was satisfactory. "If," said Vanessa, "slightly monastic, but I suppose that's logical at my age."

From the living room, which had a sort of comfortable antique-shop atmosphere, all evidence of Shadow had vanished—his pillow, his afghan, which Amy Irvington had knitted for him, his leash; and from the kitchen, the dishes for food and water, even the special Spode saucer from which at dinner time Shadow had lapped his alcoholic aperitif. Vanessa was at once aware of all this. She said, "Thanks, Stacy," and smiled. "You couldn't throw out the furniture or the window ledges or the back porch railing, I know."

Stacy said, "I kept his silver bell, for myself, Van. Do you mind?"

"You gave it to him," Vanessa said, "and, to be candid, he never liked it. But he was a gentleman and liked you, so he suffered it."

She remembered the Christmas that Stacy had given it to Shadow with a card reading, "This is for the birds."

Presently Stacy said firmly, "You have to rest."

"It seems so stupid to have my life alter in this way," Vanessa retorted.

12

"I know."

"Where are you going?"

"To the Barker farm, to talk to Angie."

"Whatever for?"

"You know she's an LPN," Stacy said. "She can't work regularly in the hospital or at someone's home because of her father's stroke."

"His own fault. He got mad and yelled at people. He has for years. That's why he keeps a dog as belligerent as he is. Well, go on—why?"

"As long as you need her she'll come down and give you injections."

"I'm not having any. Who wants artificial vigor at my age?"

"Most everyone," said Stacy.

"I can't afford her."

"Nonsense."

"You mean Warren, I suppose. Angelica—that's her name, isn't it?—is handsome," Vanessa recalled. "All the Barkers, including Angie's ill-tempered progenitor look like the aristocracy. Where do you suppose that came from? Will she also whip up little custards, tapiocas, and eggnogs for me? God forbid," she added piously.

"No. Edna's quite capable."

"Have you been in touch with Adam?"

"Yesterday. He'll be along tomorrow."

"You look peaked," Vanessa said. "Been wearing yourself out, I daresay. Lee will kill me. Go on home. I'll take a nap, Edna can stand guard. I won't try to thank you, Stacy."

Stacy went home and Cora, who had been part of Lee Osborne's household for years, said, "You look dragged down."

At dinner, which Stacy hardly touched, her husband asked, "What's wrong, darling?"

"Nothing; or maybe the heat. I wish Van's house were air-conditioned."

"It's solidly built," he said, "and she has shutters, shades, and fans. She'll be all right and it isn't that hot. So what's wrong?"

"I'm probably just tired," said Stacy. "I'll go see Bing."

"Call him tonight," Lee ordered. "Don't wait till the office is open."

She called and Bing said, "Come at ten. I don't know what Elvira has booked, but I'll surely be back from the hospital by then. Incidentally, I stopped to see Van. She's doing fine. I should be amazed, but I'm not. You've been a great help to her, Stacy. No wonder you're tired. See you tomorrow."

"So she made an appointment," Letty concluded when Bing told her of Stacy's call. "I knew she would."

"Don't look so complacent."

"It's just my natural serenity." Letty, who was knitting added, "I drop stitches. It's my glasses; I hate them."

"You'll grow accustomed," her husband promised. "You were getting as blind as they tell us love is—not that I believe that. I was astonished when at Cynthia's you discerned all by yourself that Willie was a boy. Anyway, I think you look fetching in eyeglasses. I've worn 'em for years for reading."

"They're becoming to most men," she informed him,

"and give them that statesman-owl expression. Not so with women. Me, I mislay mine. I can't find them unless I'm wearing them. I run Pearl ragged looking for them. Anyway, to save everybody's sanity, I've ordered two more pairs so I'll have one for upstairs, one for down, and an extra."

"At current prices!"

Letty looked over her glasses. "The better to see you with, Grandpa," she explained.

2

Adam Steele drove into Little Oxford down his grandmother's street, parked outside the charcoal house with the red door, descended from his small, economical secondhand car, ran up the front steps, knocked, and walked in. Edna was there. She said, "Mrs. Steele's resting now.... Have you had lunch?"

"After a fashion. Enough anyway."

"I made up the guest room"—she looked at him anxiously—"but Mrs. Steele didn't tell me to—"

"No need. I'm moving into the Osborne studio."

Vanessa called from her new quarters, "Adam?"

"What other man would drive up here on a hot June day?" he answered.

"She's in what she used to call the catchall," Edna said.

Adam went in, a tall, lean young man, with dark hair cut shorter than it once had been, his eyes the color of his grandmother's, his long face tanned. His nose

16

was a male replica of hers; his mouth and jaw his own. He said, "So the catchall finally caught you."

Vanessa was lying on the bed wearing a Hawaiian muumuu presented to her by her friend Maggie Comstock. It was, to say the least, colorful. Adam straddled a straight chair. "You look like a Xeroxed copy of yourself. Stacy told me about the arrangements and restrictions. I'll have to keep a severe eye on you."

"Suppose you tell me about your arrangements? Bing said you were renting the Osborne studio. Why? It can't be all grandfilial love."

"It isn't. I'm fed up with the Big Apple, and my father's business, so I rented the studio—it's only a spit and a holler away, Gran—and I'm going to look for a job."

"Where? There still aren't too many, and you can't march in yesteryear's bicentennial parades."

"I thought Si Westcott might have a job on the weekly *Beacon*. Maybe advertising. I can sell, you know. I sold pubs, bars, high schools, and colleges on the combo, which wasn't all that great," Adam said. "Do I smell cigar smoke?"

"Faintly. I tried it when no one was looking. Made me cough, so I quit. The witch doctors were right. I didn't hear Blasphemous, your motocycle."

"I don't have it. I have a car, a poor thing but mine own. I'll take you out in it when you're better. We'll explore the territory. Most of the natives are friendly."

"What do your parents think of this absence?"

"Dad is livid. Mom, of course, just cries, but my boss, a vice-president, let me go without argument. You are

17

perfectly aware of my current financial situation, the fund left me by my grandfather, whom I remember quite unfavorably, I might add."

"But to whom you owe an obligation."

"That's never kept anyone from disliking those they're obliged to, Gran. Anyway, until I'm thirty, the bread won't slice to caviar, a Mercedes-Benz, a suite at the Inn, or costly girls. So I'll supplement it.... Bing warned me not to tire you. You're beginning to look fragile."

"You'd tire anyone," said Vanessa. "All that energy—you exude it. But I'm glad you're here. Shall I call Si? Or maybe Katie Palmer should; she's one of his favorites."

"Thanks, no. I'll do my own dirty work. I'll just walk in and demand an audience."

"There's a new editor; Si's son was killed in a plane crash. Remember? Why won't you live with me, Adam? You'd save money."

"No, for if I did I'd pay you lavishly. Besides, I need my own pad. Commuting as I did for a year to that Early Shirley Temple parental mansion damned near drove me to drink or suicide or both. Also, I'll be entertaining—I am of course, always entertaining—but in this instance I mean as a host."

"Girls?"

"Check."

"Toby?" asked his grandmother. "I don't know her given name, the girl you brought here once—with the streaked yellow hair and astonishing makeup. I've never forgotten the flower garden embroidered on the seat of her pants. Do you still see her?"

"Occasionally. She was studying for the stage then, remember?"

"Who could forget?"

"Well, she made it; a walk-on or bit part off Broadway and in TV. She's not bad really. Her name's Sandra at present."

"What was it orginally?"

"Mary Ann Markham, but she was usually called Toby.... I'll go get settled in the studio now. Stacy's asked me to dinner. How in the world did they get Mrs. Warner to sell her house?"

"The domino theory. The Morrison house sold to a family with seven children—do you remember Abby Morrison Allen and her granddaughter Sara?"

"Of course."

"Well, now that Sara is married to Sam Peters, and they have an apartment off Parsonage Hill—downstairs, with a garden—her grandmother and Emily Warner bought a condominium together up on Lafayette Street. I told you at the time."

"I rarely listen," Adam admitted. "I just look interested. But if Westcott hires me, I'll listen like crazy on the streets, in bistros, and supermarkets."

"I doubt if he'd consent to a gossip column."

"I'd only be taking Little Oxford's pulse." Adam got off the chair. "You and Edna have the studio phone number?... Good. I'll see you tomorrow. Stay on that bed," he said, "until Edna calls you. You've had enough excitement for today."

"From doing what?"

19

"Seeing me."

At the open door he paused and said, "I miss Shadow too, Gran. May I—"

"Don't say it," she advised sharply. "Everyone's offered to find me a cat from Burmese to Siamese, Abyssinian, or alley."

"Okay.... Sure you have that number?"

"It's listed under Osborne Studio. When my telephone was put in, against my better judgment, Stacy still lived there; she gave me the number. Now get going. Give Stacy and Lee my love, and tell them I couldn't have managed without them. When *I* tell them, they pretend not to hear me."

Adam departed, and Vanessa heard him laughing with Edna in the living room. She thought: I mustn't let him know how much this means to me. He'll think I'm senile and maybe I am. For some years I've been depending on other people, Stacy mainly; now, Adam. But I never had a family until Adam was born, she told herself—dismissing her son, his wife, and of course, her former husband—everyone except Shadow.

In a few days she would be able to walk with Adam across the fields to the stone wall....

Adam drove the short distance to the studio on Lessing Lane. The only place to park was in the small circular driveway. The Wreck (short for Wreck of the Hesperus) would have to live outdoors. He wondered if the Osbornes intended to sell the studio and hoped not. If he were destiny's tot and latched on to gainful employment, perhaps he could obtain a long lease and talk Lee Osborne into building a carport, provided that,

20

by then, he could swap the Wreck for something middle-aged.

He found his key, went in, and looked about him. He'd been in the studio before Stacy had married its owner. It had been perfect for her, the bedroom, the living room and fireplace, the cathedral ceiling and the skylight. He had also been here more recently when Sam Peters had it, after Lee had added the cubbyhole guest room.

He unpacked, put away the staples he'd bought, including various bottles, in the kitchen cabinets. He'd taken nothing from his rooms at home except a portfolio filled with snapshots and memorable moments— girls, the combo, and Europe—and several gargantuan ashtrays, his clothes—he could collect his winter things at the suitable time—and his stereo and records. He'd left his big TV set at his parents' home; maybe he'd buy a small one later. Prowling about, he decided he liked the kitchen counter. Everything he needed was there—stainless-steel pots, pans, china, glasses, and adequate electrical appliances.

Super landlords, he thought, rearranging things and admiring one of Stacy's unusual paintings over the fireplace. He put the portfolio on the coffee table. If guests found it boring, too bad; but it was better than home movies. He found a place where the TV could live if it materialized, installed the stereo, and finally showered, dressed, locked up, and strolled across the fields to the Osborne house. Who'd even buy it? he wondered. It's as big as the Morrison heap, very Victorian. Not every real estate agent found clients with seven chil-

21

dren, all of whom would be living at home!

Stacy admitted him and said, "The side porch is shady and cool. Let's sit there. Lee will be down shortly. How's Van?"

"Not quite her old self; well, old, of course, but restrained. It scares me."

"Shadow," diagnosed Stacy, "and the humiliation of having been ill...Why didn't you wear shorts?"

"I shall next time."

"Have you tried your little patio yet?...No?...It's better evenings, after the flagstones have cooled off. I hope you'll be happy there, Adam. I know you'll be good for Van."

"I sure as hell hope so, and I'm going to look for a job."

"What kind?"

"I thought on the *Beacon.* If they need an office boy *cum* someone to cover music and maybe sell advertising."

Stacy said, "Well, good luck. It would have been nice having you for a neighbor, but we're moving to Emily's house in August."

Lee came down wearing shorts and a green shirt. His young face and premature white hair never ceased to fascinate Adam. He said, "Hi, youthful tenant, what are you drinking?"

They had drinks on the porch and Adam said, "I hope you aren't selling the studio."

"No way," Lee said emphatically. "We'll keep it and the two acres. I'm sentimental. My father built it for me. Stacy has an affection for it too"—he smiled at his wife—"so we rent it to people we like. Stacy had it, then Sam Peters, now you. You took a year's lease. Why?"

"Possible job," Adam said. "What about this house?" he asked.

"Not for sale. People have inquired, Emily and Katie Palmer report, but one couple wanted it for a nursing home, another for a nursery school, and there was one Katie insisted was a gangster. In any event, we won't sell to anyone. The place belongs equally to me and my sister Marcia, who lives in Texas. Last time I saw her— Stacy and I flew down some months ago—we decided to tear this down and build two ranch-type houses. The Planning and Zoning Board has consented. There are over eight acres and room for tennis courts—everyone has gone ape over tennis. I'm not bad myself," he said. "Can you play?"

"If I gave all my time to it I'd be a pro," Adam said immodestly. "I also play golf, but I can't afford the Country Club."

"There's a new one," Lee told him. "The powers decided that they'd have to consider the young and less affluent."

During dinner Adam asked, "Do you think Edna can manage with Gran?"

"She'll have help, I hope," Stacy told him, "the oldest Barker girl, Angie, an LPN, lives at home and looks after her father, but she can pop in when needed. You know the Barkers—at the farm?"

"No, but I used to admire one of the girls fervently and aloud when she walked past Gran's."

"Probably Angie.... Can you cook?"

"Camp-style and convenience foods, enough to keep body and soul together, and there are always the diner and the small bistros. I'll get along fine."

"You certainly will," Lee remarked. "There are few eligible bachelors around as of now. Just the teenagers and college students, who will have to grow up. When Matt Comstock married there was a ground swell of disappointment, but then Sam Peters came along. Now he's married. You can dine out every night if you like," Lee told his tenant, "once the word gets around. Independent young women and frantic hostesses with unattached female guests will start laying traps."

"He should know," his wife remarked. "He was a bachelor for a long time."

Adam left early, but when he reached the studio decided it was a good evening for walking. All he did, however, was to go by his grandmother's and look. A light burned upstairs. Edna's? Van was in her own room then and, he hoped, sleeping.

He yawned, went back to the studio, and called Toby Markham. She was resting, as the euphemism goes, at her parents' home, between engagements. In the city she shared an apartment with three other girls—an apprentice designer, a ballet student, and a model—but the walk-up was not air-conditioned and the Westchester house was.

"Toby. So what's new?"

She said, in a voice less affected than when Vanessa had met her, "Superboring of course; I trek in and out of town for auditions. I may land a TV commercial."

"I hope it's something the kiddies can see."

24

"Not exactly. My anxious parents will be struck by bolt lightning if I get it and, as a matter of fact," said Toby, "as long as I'm not starving maybe I won't even audition."

"How about coming up to Little Oxford this weekend, provided you still have a car."

"Of course I have a car. It's here, not in town.... How's your grandmother?"

"Doing very well."

"Will you have to take me to see her?"

"No. Why?"

"She scares me, and her cat does too."

"She no longer has her cat," he assured her, "but I'll go alone and I'll give her your regards."

"You'll tell her I'm staying with you?"

"Naturally."

"She'll disinherit you," Toby warned him.

"She can't. To paraphrase an old song, her trust is my trust, eventually, but I hope she'll live forever; if you're nursing the fancy that my grandmother would have the vapors, she was liberated a long, long time ago."

When he hung up, he was smiling, remembering a conversation he had had with Vanessa when he was sixteen. He couldn't talk to his mother or his father, who, when Adam was thirteen, had tried to advise him but had succeeded only in embarrassing them both. So he'd wound up one weekend talking with his grandmother. He remembered it all, but especially how, regarding him with her astonishing eyes while Shadow sat on a bookcase and smiled, she'd said, "Every generation firmly believes it invented sex, which is not to say love. They're sometimes related of course, if not always. You'll discover that love—however poor in substance, however temporary—is not an invention. Poets and philosophers have tried to define it and failed. There'll be a number of times when you'll be in love—small *l*—but I hope you eventually find it with a capital *L.*

"Looking back—which is like twisting your neck, it leaves a wryness in your mind—I think I experienced it once.... I'm not really sure now," said Vanessa.

Adam thought: That capital *L* can wait. In his present circumstances he couldn't afford to be what's known as "serious."

Today was Thursday. Tomorrow afternoon Toby would arrive in the car that had been provided by her doting, if square, parents. They had always encouraged her association with Adam. He had been almost a neighbor and his background was respectable, barring an eccentric grandmother. But everyone had at least one strange bird nesting in the family tree.

When they learned about Toby's weekend plans, they would assure themselves that she'd be chaperoned; even an eccentric grandmother is acceptable in such a situation.

Tomorrow Adam would look in his kitchen cupboards and refrigerator. He was a better cook than Toby. Saturday night he'd take her out someplace where they could dance. And during the day they could swim in Mrs. Nile's pool. Stacy had told him that Mrs. Niles was in Europe, but that the pool was available to her friends. "The caretaker checks," Stacy had said, "but you're a favorite of Rosie's, so if you have weekend playmates, call up Jim Preston. He's been caretaker there for years; you must know him."

In addition to Mrs. Niles's fabulous pool, there was, within a short driving distance, salt water, a public beach, and sailboats scudding or drifting against the sky. He said a short prayer. No rain, no sudden thunder, for to be housebound with Miss Markham was not his idea of paradise.

After shopping next morning, Adam went to the Niles house and spoke to Jim Preston. Jim, gnarled as an old apple tree, with cloudless blue eyes and a face carved from mahogany, remembered Adam and said he'd be welcome. The pool was always clean, fresh, and properly cared for. "Just no carryings-on," Jim reminded him. "That's Mrs. Niles's one condition. She don't want to come back to no lawsuits."

On his way home Adam stopped to see Vanessa. Going in the back way, he was met by Edna and a tall young woman, whose eyes were almost on a level with his own. Edna said, "Angie, this is Adam, Mrs. Steele's grandson."

They shook hands and Adam imagined that, if need be, Angie's grip could be pitiless. "I think I've seen you a time or two," he told her, "walking down the road."

"From the Barker farm," she agreed. She looked at Edna and said. "I have to get back home now, but I'll be here this evening, about eight."

"How's Gran?" Adam asked and Angie answered, "Fine, though of course she resents her inactivity. Dr. Irvington will be in to see her this afternoon." She

27

smiled and added, "Call me if anything disturbs you, Edna."

She left, and Adam went in to see Vanessa, who said, "I hate this room. I used to like it when it was full of things I was too lazy to get rid of. It's been tidied up, but there's still some trash."

Adam looked around. It was unusually neat. "Meaning yourself?" he asked.

"Not quite. I'm not good enough to keep but too good to throw out," she told him. She looked better. Her eyes were bright, and there was color under her brown skin.

"Did you see Angie?"

"Yes indeed. She's something else."

"Hands off," Vanessa warned him. "She has a follower."

"How do you know?"

"She told me. I always ask. It's the only way."

"He must be a salesman," Adam deduced.

"Is that old gag still around? No. He's a resident at the hospital, and all the things you're not."

"Such as?"

"Clever, studious, serious, useful, and concerned."

"Any personality?"

"Enough."

"Did she bring him to see you?"

"No. I saw him when I was in the hospital. He asked me if I knew her. You stick to the Tobys of this fearsome world."

Adam rose and kissed her lined, brown cheek. "Illustrious ancestress, I'm not really interested in any

28

woman, just all women. Besides, the farmer's daughter intimidates me," he said.

"Unimaginable. Why?"

"Give her another inch and she'd tower over me. What's my unrival's name?"

"You won't believe it."

"Try me."

"Dr. Wright.... Don't bring Toby to see me. I'm still in a delicate condition."

"She wouldn't come; you scare her."

"Good. I can still cast spells. Bing's coming this afternoon. I think in another week I'll be able to take the stairs more often, and go outdoors before the first snow. Then I want you to take me for a short walk.... When are you going to storm the Westcott office?"

"Monday. See you tomorrow sometime."

She watched him go, smiling, and thought, not for the first time that young people give their elders a certain amount of energy, except of course for certain types who drain you. Adam was a giver, she thought, as Edna came in with the lunch tray, settled the pillows behind her back, and said, "You must eat something, Mrs. Steele. You've lost more weight."

"I'll try, and thank you," said Vanessa, for Edna did her best.

Adam drove to the studio. With all the groceries and other packages, he had to drive, even though the Wreck consumed each refill as if it were her last, as indeed it might be. On the way he reflected upon Angie Barker. She and Toby were about the same height, but there the resemblance ended. Angie had long corn-colored hair which she wore coiled at the back. Her eyes were gray, her fair skin slightly freckled, and she had a generous mouth, which curved upward. She was not fashionably thin, but neither was she overweight. She had, he suspected, plenty of muscle, and wondered if her doctor did also.

Adam thought: Someday I'll just look up and see my personal heart stopper. She'd be small in latitude and longitude with, he sometimes thought, auburn hair—was there still such a color?—and green eyes. He'd never found her and often he altered the specifications; but she still stayed where she had been born—in his mind.

3

Toby buzzed up like a hornet in her costly car that rather looked like one; it was brown with yellow stripes. Adam standing in the driveway, remarked, "As usual, you're late."

"Lousy directions," she said reproachfully, waving a slip of paper at him. "I was lost three times, I nearly got a ticket and had to summon all my helpless charm."

"You are always more lost than found. Do alight."

"My suitcase."

He took it. "You need all that for a weekend?"

"One never knows. I even brought a bathing suit."

"It's too cold to swim yet in fresh or salt water."

"Is that your heap?" she inquired, indicating Adam's vehicle.

"It is."

"Where's the garage?"

"There isn't any."

"We could be ripped off."

31

"Not likely in this neighborhood. My witchcraft grandmother's right around the corner. Little Oxford does have vandals, burglaries, freaked-out citizens, and the like, but so far no significant invasion of privacy hereabouts."

He marched her into the studio, and Toby commented, "Reasonably attractive. I like the furniture, but why a skylight?"

"My landlord used the studio once; he's an architect. By the way, I'm putting you in my bedroom."

"Naturally," Toby agreed, raising an eyebrow.

"There's a guest room. Lee Osborne, the landlord—architect, added it a while back." He showed Toby the small, practical cubicle, complete with single bed, built-in bureau drawers, good lighting, small radio, and two closets, one of which contained a shower. "Very ship-shape," he said.

"Claustrophobia, pure and simple," Toby remarked.

"Nonsense, look at the two windows."

"Why? Thank God, I won't have to sleep there." She strolled into the other bedroom. "The master will be just fine," she told him, and looked at the watch which glittered on her wrist. "It's time," she informed him, "for the relaxing exercise known as the social hour, after I've unpacked and renovated my face."

"Of course, and you needn't slip into something comfortable," Adam said.

She wore short shorts, a rainbow-striped mesh jacket that ended just above her navel, and platform shoes.

"You know how it was at home," she reminded him.

"We were taught to dress for dinner even when the natives were restless."

Adam went to make the aperitifs, smiling. He was mildly attached to Toby, originally because she was almost two years his senior. When he was fourteen, she had been an older woman. Bu why the hell had he asked her here, he wondered. He hadn't seen her in a long time. Running into her at a bash a month ago or more didn't explain it. And I'm not bored, he told himself. I haven't had time to be.

Toby floated out in a sheer blue garment, her hair piled on top of her head, and her bare brown legs ending in sandals. "How do you stay tanned all year?" he asked.

She inserted herself into a corner of a love seat and answered dreamily, "Oh, I have a sun lamp and then I was in Florida to rest and in the Bahamas on a yacht."

"Resting from what?"

"Everything.... Thanks," she added, taking the glass he gave her. "From work, whenever I had it briefly, from the other girls in the apartment. Big deal. All of us usually wanted it alone, on the same nights. Also we had to do our share of housework. Revolting."

"How about some crackers and cheese?"

"I never eat with a drink," she told him. "Also I was resting from the parents. Incidentally, I didn't get that commercial. I'll return to town Sunday, start the rounds Monday. I hear they're looking for a pretty girl to do a dog-food commercial and don't say what you're thinking. The dog is, of course, the star."

"What do your parents think of your current life-style?" Adam asked, sitting down opposite her.

"They try not to think," she answered. "They listen to what I tell them; they know where I am when I go away, but not much more. They don't want to know. I'm sorry for parents of wayward children who are of legal age."

"They worry more about daughters than sons," Adam said.

"Tell that to Gloria Steinem," she suggested. "What's for dinner? Are we going out or will you cook?... I remember you did the first and only time you came to the apartment. Ginger was there, and Holly. They thought you were cute."

"Thanks. I am, in the original sense of the word. Dinner isn't far off, in this age of convenience foods. The entrée needs only a short sojourn in the oven. I put it there when I made the drinks. There's a salad in the fridge, a bottle of wine, silver and china in the cupboards, paper napkins beneath the counter. Would you care to assist me?"

"No."

"We dine," he told her, "at the counter, on stools."

"How about a refresher?" she asked, pointing a long finger at her glass.

"Kills the taste buds."

Toby scowled. "You told me when I last saw you that I'd improved. In what way?"

"Physically. Your hair's a credible color, and I fancy you brush it more often. Also the makeup's less obvious."

34

"Thanks.... I'm hungry. When do we eat?"

"Now. Try to stay on the stool."

Afterward, Adam washed up while Toby reclined on the love seat with a tot of brandy and listened to the hi-fi.

"You'll make some lucky girl a great wife," she said. "Do you realize my sacrifice in refusing ice cream? The camera adds pounds.... Why ever did you come here, Adam?"

"To be near Grandmother."

"Don't be absurd. Practically no one wants to be near their grandmothers. I have two, one's short, fat, and tearful; the other's long, thin, and military. There must be a girl-person in your rustic woodpile."

"Negative. My favorite girls are working in various localities, off to resorts, in this country or others, or undertaking serious summer studies."

"But what will you *do* here?"

"I hope to go to work."

"But you have a job."

"I resigned. They didn't hate to see me go."

"What can you do?"

"Suffice it to say I couldn't do what I was supposed to be doing with any degree of success or enthusiasm. If I don't get a regular job, consider my assets. I can tend bar, wait tables, mow lawns, make simple repairs, manage a combo—"

"Sounds dreadful. Come over here and sit by me."

He obeyed and put his arm around her. She asked, "Were you ever in love with me?"

"Hopelessly, when I was fourteen, and still somewhat when we came here the last time. Remember, we stopped at Gran's and went for a swim and a picnic?"

"Your grandmother didn't approve of me."

"Correction. Disapproval takes too much energy. Besides, she's only curious about people; she rarely judges them."

"I don't really like brandy," Toby said. "How about a gin and tonic?"

He brought it to her, remarking, "You'll destroy your skin, your figure, and career."

"They're all mine," she reminded him. "You're not involved." After a moment, she added, "You're acting all noble, Adam. It's unbecoming. Do sit down. You're making me nervous, pacing like an expectant father."

Adam obediently sat across from her on the other love seat and Toby said, "I don't bite.... You didn't bring your drink."

"I left it where I prefer it, in a bottle."

She pushed her hair from her forehead and sighed. "What's the big idea? You sound like my father," she complained.

"Well," Adam told her, "I like you. I don't enjoy seeing you being stupid."

"You're as stuffy as your parents and mine. Know something? I resort to alcohol when I'm bored, lonely, angry, or don't like whom I'm with."

The telephone rang. Adam went to answer and Toby heard him say, "Edna? Everything okay... I'll be in tomorrow."

When he returned. Toby asked, "So who's Edna?"

"She looks after Gran and calls me about this time every evening."

"Don't you ever go out?"

"Naturally. In that case I call her when I come back."

"Well, really!" said Toby in a sleepy, but exasperated voice. Then she brightened, "So you're Granny's heir."

"Yes, but that was settled many years ago and she had nothing to say about it."

Toby was silent; she had fallen asleep.

Presently Adam picked her up, carried her into his room, laid her on the bed, and rummaged through her unpacked suitcase. The last drink had been long on tonic, short on gin, but Toby was as limp as a rag doll. She had told him once that she hated dolls, except for a clown doll she'd kept since childhood. His name was Toby, and she'd also taken the name herself.

Adam undressed her, put a nightgown on her thin, almost wholly tanned body, placed a light blanket over her, raised a window, and went back to the living room, leaving the bedroom door open.

He had taken a small bottle from Toby's suitcase. Now he regarded it thoughtfully for a moment and then called Ben Irvington. Amy answered. "It's Adam," he said. "Sorry to call this late. Is Ben home?"

"It isn't late for us. I'll get him."

When Ben came to the phone, Adam said, "I have a girl visitor and I've just put her to bed. She passed out."

"How much has she had to drink?"

Adam told him, adding, "But it wasn't much for her—enough to get high, perhaps. However, I found a prescription drug in her bag."

"Read me the label."

Adam did and Ben said, "A tranquilizer. She probably took it before dinner.... You did have dinner? Try to wake her. If you can't, call me back at once."

Adam returned to the bedroom. He spoke urgently to Toby, then wiped her face with a cold wet cloth.

She finally opened her eyes and muttered, "If you're trying to seduce me, it's the wrong method."

"You've taken tranquilizers."

"How'd you know?... Oh—snooping? Leave me alone unless you have something interesting to suggest," she said sleepily. "Otherwise, scram."

"I just talked to my doctor."

"Go back and talk some more," said Toby. "I'll be fine in the morning. Just let me sleep."

Adam spent most of the night listening. He heard his guest turn, mutter, and occasionally snore. Now and then he went in to check on her—quietly.

In the morning, she woke him. She asked, at the guest room door, "Did you put my nightgown on me?"

"Yes."

"How enterprising!...I make bad coffee. You try."

"In a few minutes. You go back to bed. I'll bring it to you."

He brought it on a tray. She looked fine, if a little disheveled, and said, "I could do with a Bloody Mary."

"I'm sure you could. Just drink the coffee." He sat

down on the bed and looked at her propped up against the pillows.

"Don't lecture," she advised, yawning. "Let's go somewhere and take a picnic."

"No picnic; it's going to rain," he told her. "Toby, do you often do what you did last night?"

"What did I do?"

"You passed out."

"Oh that," she said carelessly. "No, not often. Sorry I inconvenienced you."

"Your explanation wasn't convincing. Why do you drink?"

"What did I say?... May I have more coffee?"

"Sure." He took her cup and refilled it.

"You said you drank when you were bored, lonely, angry, or didn't like whom you were with."

"Well," she said triumphantly, "I *was* bored. I came here expecting a little excitement, so I was mad at you. As for being lonely, I am, always."

"And you don't like me very much."

"That one's not true. I do like you most of the time, but you irritate me. Always the boy next door, the good guy."

"Toby, when I woke you, you were coherent, if fuzzy, and talking, as if through a mouthful of cotton. Why don't you tell me what really drives you to drink and drugs?"

"Men," she said. "Since I was fourteen and you were twelve. I had heroes, but mostly they were in Hollywood. I had fantasies. I still have fantasies, but I've never found anyone.... God knows I've tried—young, old, fat, thin, married, single. Funny thing, the only man I've ever known who I thought was on my wavelength didn't like women."

"Sometimes," Adam said, "if you stop looking—"

"A lot you know about it.... Where are you going?"

"I'm walking over to Gran's." He took the empty cup. "When I come back, we'll have lunch, go for a drive and later I'll take you to a good Greek restaurant for dinner.... Would you like toast and an egg before I go?"

She made a hideous face.

"Very well..." He hesitated, then said, "Toby, you should see a doctor."

"No thanks. The last one I saw had been a football player in college, so he knew all about passes—in a discreet way, of course. And I don't need a shrink. I just hate living and I'm terrified of dying," she said.

Someday, he thought, walking to Vanessa's, she may grow up.

His grandmother was downstairs, with Angie Barker, and Edna was in the kitchen. "Lunch?" asked Vanessa. "Oh, I forgot you have a visitor. How is she?"

"As well as can be expected," he answered gravely and looked at Angie, who was smiling. Tall, with corn-colored hair, gray eyes, scattered freckles. He wondered what her Dr. Wright was like.

"I'm going now," Angie said. "I'll be in again at eight, Mrs. Steele."

"Thanks....Tell your mother to come see me sometime."

When she'd gone, Vanessa said, "You don't look quite the thing, as a friend of mine used to say. Trouble with the guest?"

"Not really."

"Barkis wasn't willing?"

He laughed. "I suppose in other circumstances he might have been."

"How many circumstances are there? Let me see. She doesn't really attract you; or she has tantrums; she refused you; or one of you had too much to drink." She looked at him with the still unfaded eyes, and then put on her glasses. "It wasn't you. I've known you since you had your first, and at that time, illegal, drink."

"Gran," he said, "something's very wrong with Toby. She needs medical help."

Vanessa made an impatient sound and said in the deep voice very little altered by age, "So you're sorry for her."

"Of course."

"Get over it. There's nothing more frustrating, useless, and dangerous. Pity's a trap."

Edna appeared announcing, "Mrs. Osborne's here."

Stacy came in, her long black hair flying. She said, "Guess what?"

"You're pregnant," Vanessa said.

Young Mrs. Osborne sat down amid the clutter on a long hassock, "Damn and blast!" she said.

"Why?" asked Adam, entertained.

41

"Letty Irvington knew. Van knew. How come? I'm as thin as an excuse. I don't get nauseous. I have no fancy for pickles. I feel great."

"It's just a certain look," Vanessa said. "Are you and Lee happy about it?"

"Ecstatic. Of course there are a few problems."

"Such as?" Adam asked.

"Well, I want to get moved before I'm in the zeppelin stage and there's so much to do: shipping Marcia's things, though she doesn't want much; a garage sale; and selecting what we want to take with us. Emily's house is partially furnished; she didn't take everything to the condominium."

"I'll run your garage sale," Adam offered. "Though I'm not an appraiser, I once helped a friend's mother, and women are always easier prey when there's a man salesman."

"Still a chauvinist," Stacy said. "But, thanks."

"What else is worrisome?" Vanessa asked.

"Lee treats me as if I were a Grecian urn. There's also the question of names. I don't want a second Anastasia, so I've decided with your permission, on yours, Van."

"Be my guest," Vanessa said courteously. "What have I done to deserve this?"

"Just brought me all the good fortune I've ever known—Lee, for instance."

"Suppose you have a boy?" Adam asked.

"Then it's easy," Stacy said. "Well, I have to go. Cora and I have things to do and besides Lee phones twice a day when he isn't coming to lunch, which is idiotic.

I'm extremely healthy and intend to remain that way."

When she'd left, Vanessa remarked, "She wasn't always so happy and healthy, you know. She had a rough time before Little Oxford took over."

Adam kissed the top of her head. "Have Edna or Angie call me tonight. I'd better get back to Toby."

But when he reached the studio, the "hornet" was gone and there was a note on the coffee table: "I'm going back to town," Toby had scrawled. "Thanks for everything. I don't feel up to a country tour or Greek dinners or to being cooped up in the rain. Love, Toby."

Adam felt guilty because he was so relieved.

4

Thoughtfully, Adam contemplated the immediate future. He was now a free agent. Saturday night? Everyone he knew would have other engagements; anyway the majority were married. Very well, he'd take himself out to dinner.

He telephoned the Aegean and made a reservation. He had been there a number of times—once, some years ago he'd gone with his grandmother and the Osbornes. Tonight, there would be dancing. He would sit, solitary at a table, still feeling guilty, but otherwise happy. He'd have a chat with Theodorus and his wife Thalia. He'd order rosé and, having learned from Lee Osborne, the *avgolemono* and the *moussaka*.

He arrived at the restaurant on the stroke of six and was greeted by Thalia. "It isn't possible," she said.

"Anything is, but in this case, what?"

"You're alone."

"But not lonely," he assured her. "How are Cherry and her husband?"

"Fine; she's having a baby. She's returned to her baptismal name, Charis, since she's discovered it attracts attention.... Will this be all right, Adam?"

"Splendid," he answered, sitting down at a corner table and lifting a hand in greeting to the owner who was coming toward them. "How's Alexis, Theo?"

"Graduated," Theo said smiling, "and serving an apprenticeship here for the summer; but he's off tonight. How's your grandmother? Lee told me of her regrettable illness."

"She's recovering, grumpily."

"She likes our olives and the bread we bake so, with your permission, I'll send her some of both.... Let me take your order. Our current waitress is occupied. We've been fortunate in getting capable girls since Charis left, but there's something fatal about this place; they all marry within a year."

"I'm glad the hex applies only to females," Adam said. "I'm in the process of celebrating all my escapes."

"Knock wood," Thalia advised. "Very few can run fast enough."

He had almost finished and was drinking Greek coffee, eating *baklava*, and watching people dance to the jukebox music, when Stacy and Lee Osborne came in with a young woman. They did not see him and Adam regarded their guest with gratified amazement. She was small, rounded in the correct places, and her hair—which was the color he thought of as auburn—cascaded over her shoulders, held back by a velvet band. He could not see her face properly, just the curve of a cheek, the shadow of eyelashes, so he sat staring at her hair, her back being toward him, until Stacy waved, and Lee rose and came over. "You should have phoned to let us know you were alone," he said, "and come with us. Join us now for coffee."

"And what's left of the wine," Adam said, "which I hope you'll drink.... Thanks, Lee. I hope I won't be intruding."

"Nonsense." Lee beckoned and Theo came up. "Do give Adam fresh coffee at our table," Lee suggested, "as he's donating his wine."

"Who's the gorgeous girl?" Adam asked, as they crossed the room.

"Carol Benson. She's related to Si Westcott's wife and came from upstate in April to work on the paper."

"I don't believe it," Adam murmured.

Lee asked mildly, "Why not? She worked on her hometown daily after graduating in journalism."

They'd reached the Osborne table. The waitress set the fourth place, brought a chair, and introductions were made.

Seen across a table, the girl with the long red-gold hair had hazel eyes, fair skin, a slightly snub nose, and a cleft in her chin. She asked, amused, "Do I remind you of someone, Mr. Steele?"

"Oh, yes," Adam answered, recovering. "Someone I've known for a long time but haven't met until now."

"Pay him no mind," suggested Stacy. "He only does it to annoy—because he knows it teases."

Carol Benson looked politely puzzled. Adam's coffee

and wine arrived and they all drank the rosé. Adam had had only a glass, and there was still enough to go around.

Lee asked, "How come you're alone?"

"My weekend guest fled back to town before I could ply her with various Greek intoxicants." He looked at Carol and added, "Would you care to dance, Miss Benson?" He saw the ring on her left hand and his mind stumbled over an obstacle. "Mrs.?" he asked. "Ms.?"

"Carol," she said. "Miss isn't true, Mrs. was always a bore, and Ms. annoys me."

They danced. The Greek records that were also in the jukebox were not being played this evening.

Dancing, he asked, "Why haven't I met you before?"

"When did you arrive in Little Oxford?"

He told her, and added, "But I've been coming for years to my grandmother's."

"Vanessa Steele?" she asked animatedly. "Would she give me an interview?"

Adam, a flawless dancer, stumbled slightly. "Certainly not," he said. "Whatever for?"

"I've been coming here for ages too," she told him, "weekends, short holidays. My aunt lives here. My job on the *Beacon* is to do feature articles—old houses, interesting residents, that sort of thing—all part of the woman's page, which is mostly social events. It's a summer deal. I hope to go to the city in the autumn and find something permanent. This is a time killer. I went to New York in March, but there wasn't anything anywhere, so I asked Uncle Si if I could work for pocket money, lodging, and sustenance.... What do you do?"

"Nothing at present," Adam answered truthfully. "But I've had some business experience, and before that I managed a combo."

He thought: Shall I ask her if her uncle could find a use for me? No. A dozen Little Oxfordites would vouch for him, but Carol Benson couldn't; she didn't know him.

Presently they all left together, and Stacy said, "Adam, come to supper tomorrow and amuse Lee. He's terribly serious about this interruption of our happy carefree married life."

"I am not," said her husband. "It's an interruption I'll learn to enjoy. Now I'm simply afraid you'll fall downstairs."

Adam drove home. Curious that Stacy hadn't invited Carol Benson too. Then he brightened. With any luck he'd get to see her everyday, he thought.

Dinner with the Osbornes was interesting. "Cora," explained Stacy, "keeps me out of the kitchen. She says darkly, 'You have to be careful—the first three months especially. Stay off your feet,' she says and uses my indelicate condition as an excuse to try out the dandiest recipes. She gets them from health-food cookbooks, newspapers, and magazines. And if I ask her, 'What's for dinner?' she simply says, 'You'll see.' Lee's resigned to her experimentation and I must admit everything's been elegant and, for my sake, low calorie."

Cora came in with salad and said severely, "I heard."

"But it was flattering," Adam told her, "as it should be."

Later Lee said, "As the ladylike mysteries once began, 'Had I but known' that Stacy would put me through this, we wouldn't have planned to move until after the event. Incidentally, Adam, you'll be exposed to a great deal of demolition noise."

"I don't mind noise," Adam told him. "I'm a child of the fifties. Remember? I was brought up on rock and roll, experienced country and western, and the return of big bands, jazz and blues groups, then managed to oversee a good deal of noise myself. Anyway, I'll be working in the village, I hope."

"On the *Beacon*," supplemented Stacy. "Van told me.... What did you think of Carol Benson?"

"Dream girl," he told her. "Why haven't you exposed me before?"

"We didn't know her," Lee told him. "We see the Westcotts very occasionally, so we didn't meet her prior to her coming here to live. Then she came to see us. She wrote an article about us. You know the type of thing—husband and wife, architect and artist. It wasn't bad."

"It was glorious," his wife remarked, "all about my exotic beauty, your hereditary white hair, and what assets we are to the community."

"Most embarrassing," her husband remarked.

"She told me she'd like to interview Gran," Adam said.

"Good grief!" and "God forbid!" cried the Osbornes simultaneously.

"I said no dice. What do you know about this girl anyway?"

"Just the vital statistics, up till now, where she was born, what college she attended, her marriage, and her relationship to the Westcotts."

"She's divorced, I imagine," said Adam.

"Certainly," Stacy said. "I gather it was quite a different process than mine. You're taken with her, Adam. Admit it."

"Wouldn't any red-blooded man be?"

"Not necessarily," Lee replied and Stacy said, "You're too prompt with the disclaimer. Carol has to be older than you, Adam—college, the work on a daily paper, the marriage—"

"She probably entered college at sixteen," Adam said promptly, smiling. "And besides, if my memory serves, the first time I walked into your studio I told you I liked older women."

Lee said, "I haven't seen Van for a few days. Does she talk about Shadow?"

"No. I'm going to walk with her to the stone wall sometime soon. She's a lot stronger now—indestructible, she thinks. Maybe she's right."

Later, on his way back to the studio he thought about Stacy Osborne and the little he knew of her past difficulties and frustrations. He was fond of and admired her and her painting, which had steadily progressed. Vanessa was not given to public appearances, but had gone with him over a year ago to Stacy's one-woman show, her third, and had remarked, "Something's missing—the streak of melancholy, the flash of wildness—but something's been added—serenity."

Looking at his watch when he let himself in, he saw

that it was early. Stacy had yawned her way to bed saying, "I don't know why I'm so sleepy. I must be preparing myself instinctively for the long, wakeful hours."

"How about me?" inquired her husband.

"Only twins would make enough noise for you to crash out of bed and assist in whatever procedure.... Did I tell you Adam, I've enrolled in a prenatal class? Lee's promised to attend. I don't believe him."

It was now ten o'clock and Adam went to the telephone and dialed Toby in New York.

"This is Ginger, in case you're for me," someone answered.

"Hi. Adam Steele here. Is Toby around?"

"Not since she came back from your pad. This is to say, she went out on her return Saturday, came in this morning, repacked her suitcase, and flew to Sun Valley."

"Why?"

"Who knows? She said she'd met a man from Boise!"

On Monday morning Adam drove up Parsonage Hill, turned into the parking space, walked to the corner of Colonial and Pepperidge, and entered the *Beacon* Building. The front office was presided over by a young woman who took printing orders and classified ads.

"I'm Adam Steele," he told her, smiling, and she looked momentarily bemused. He often had such an effect upon females, young or old. "Do you think Mr. Westcott would see me for a few minutes?"

"I'll ask."

She spoke into an intercom, looked up, and reported, "Go right in—around the counter to the right."

Adam thanked her, found the door, knocked, and was bidden to enter. Si Westcott—portly, gray, with a young face and intrepid blue eyes—rose from behind the desk. "You're Vanessa's grandson," he said.

"That's right."

"How is she?"

"Doing very well, though that's a silly expression," Adam complained.

"You want a job," stated Si, without a question mark.

"How'd you know?"

"Rumor," Si answered, smiling. The smile didn't quite reach his eyes. He added, "Well, not exactly. Carol told me about you. Seems she'd made inquiries."

"Did she recommend me?"

"No. She knows I don't go by reference, Adam. When Slim, my son, was killed in a plane disaster, your grandmother wrote us a short letter, no platitudes, no stiff upper lip, no time will heal. An angry letter, really. You know how in certain heart cases doctors pound and shock you into taking up where you left off? Well, it was like that.... Now, what can you do exactly?"

Adam told him and after a while Si said, "How about a helper? Fill in there, fill in here, do some leg work for our advertising manager Nick Denton, cover some music and school activities—dogsbody, in other words. This is a small paper, but we have correspondents in a couple of other towns. I write editorials mostly. Carol does feature stuff. Mary O'Malley runs the woman's page and the social items and contributes an editorial now and then. So does our reporter, Tom Williams. Everybody pitches in. Summer's busy of course, as we have, as you know, summer residents and also—heaven help us!—tourists. We no longer print the *Beacon*, we have no presses—it's offset as are a couple of other area weeklies up the line at Menly, past Deeport. We can't pay much, Adam. Suppose you try out for the rest of the summer. Can you write?" he asked abruptly.

"I was an English major, which is not to say I'm any Norman Mailer or James Baldwin or even Louisa May Alcott, but I think I can manage. And I hope by fall you'll find I've been useful."

"There'll be art shows, too, at the Gallery and on the streets. I used to try to get Stacy Osborne to cover those, but she wouldn't. She claimed she'd be either envious or patronizing. Carol's been doing it. She doesn't paint, but she has a flair. Her father, my wife's brother, was an artist. Unsuccessful, but she learned something about art." He spoke on the intercom, "Send in Nick," he said.

Nicholas Denton was middle-aged, short, and nervous. "This is Adam Steele," said Westcott. "I've just hired him for, you'll be glad to hear, peanuts. He's going to do odd jobs for us—you, me, O'Malley, and Williams. We can put a desk, chair, and typewriter in your office. Mrs. O'Malley has all she can handle with Carol. So take him in, and if you both decide you can't get along with each other, let me know. I'll fire one of you—Adam of course, the last hired." He looked at Adam and once more smiled, no warmth touching the blue eyes. "Nick has a wife," he added, "a couple of kids…. That reminds me, where do you live, Adam?"

"In the Osborne studio."

"Be here tomorrow," said Si. "You'll keep mostly irregular hours when we're busy; take a half hour for lunch, there's a diner on Pepperidge. You get Saturday and Sunday off, and if you stick around, you rate two weeks vacation after a year. Paper comes out Thursdays…. Bye."

Denton's office was as big as Si's. "It was Slim's," he explained. "I shared it. We don't have a lot of space. Si used to talk of building further out, as we can't add on to this—but he hasn't since Slim's death. Haul up a chair, we'll talk. Do you know anyone in business here?" he asked.

Adam said he did: Jeremy and Sam in the bookshop, Emily Warner in real estate, Lee Osborne.

Nick shook his head. "They're all sewed up. I just use the phone to contact them. Incidentally, it wasn't till Sam Peters bought into the bookshop that Jeremy Palmer advertised. I'll give you a list. The town changes often, and it's doing so now. Shops come in or move out. You'll have to get to know people, and there'll be a lot of walking. I've always done it, but I'm getting tired and I have a bad knee. I asked Si for an assistant once; he said I was losing my mind. You haven't met Mrs. O'Malley?"

"No, just Carol."

"Carol's something to meet," said Nick. "My wife hates her, Mary O'Malley hates her, so does Tom Williams's wife. You'll be helping Tom too. He'll send you out to report on new construction and various dull

54

meetings. Si saves the town meetings for himself."

"Where's Williams's office?"

"A cubbyhole next door. He could have come in with me, but he prefers solitude. It rests his feet and nourishes his dreams—of a daily upstate, and of going eventually to the city, and after a short apprenticeship becoming the O. Henry of the era with, however, no holds or expletives barred. But you'll like him. I'll take you to meet him and O'Malley now."

Later, as Adam went back up the hill to his car, he wondered how many "peanuts" Si Westcott planned to pay him. He hadn't the slightest idea.

He went directly to his grandmother's and found her alone in the living room, seated in a big chair, her feet resting on a hassock. "What's this?" he demanded.

"Edna's gone grocery shopping on her bicycle," Vanessa explained. "Don't be mother-henish. There are phones all over the house—kitchen, living room, bedroom, as you very well know. Your father insisted." She looked thoughtful. "Duty, I suspect, and making up for the years he didn't see me. But why? His father divorced me, and in those days I wouldn't have been given custody if I'd wanted it, which I didn't. Frankly, Adam, I've never cared much for your father and had no maternal instincts whatsoever until you barged into my life —and a couple of other young people—Stacy, for instance. And I don't know that it's maternal, rather, I think, a desire to be around young people."

"Dad worries about you," Adam told her.

"If so, God knows why. I respect my son," she said,

"for his sterling qualities—I've no idea where they came from—but I dislike being grateful, which much against my will, I am. What happened at the *Beacon*?"

"I'm hired."

"As what?"

"Factotum," he told her. "I'll know more tomorrow about what I'm being paid—in 'peanuts.'"

"Very useful if you were a monkey or an elephant."

"Whatever it is, I'll get along. Even if I'm fired," Adam said.

Someone called from the back door and Angie Barker made her appearance. "Hi," she said to Adam and then, "it's time for your injection, Mrs. Steele."

Vanessa looked at her and said, "I don't know what effect you have on other old crocks, but it's illegal for anyone to look as you do, teeming with health and vitality."

"Sorry about that," Angie told her.

"Go away somewhere or at least turn your back," Vanessa told Adam. "I don't like to be observed when helpless."

He did so, walking about, and when Angie said, laughing, "You can turn around, Mr. Steele," he observed mildly. "What's wrong with Adam?"

"Everything," said his grandmother. "You know, I should get rid of some of the undergrowth in this jungle. Take anything you want."

"Nope," Adam said. "Stacy offered me a cleaning person, but I'd rather do it myself, and I have no wish to add to my burdens. The care and feeding of possessions is absurd.... Hey, who's this jolly Oriental gentleman?"

"He's the God of Happiness. Rub his teakwood belly for luck. I used to once upon a time, and occasionally he appeared to smile on my modest hopes, but more often, not."

"Suppose I try my luck? May I have him?"

"Certainly. But be careful about what you ask for, and be specific or you may get your wish in a form you'll find unfortunate."

Angie said, gathering her things together, "I'd better go now, Mrs. Steele. See you this evening." She waved her capable brown hand in farewell and smiled. "Take care," she said to them both and left.

"That's quite a girl," Adam remarked.

"She is. I thought I'd mind the physical attentions, as I did both times I was in the hospital. But with Angie I don't. She doesn't fuss; she's impersonally kind; she never says 'Time for *our* bath.' Her medic will bless the day he marries her, if indeed he does. I gather she's not cooperative. I asked her about him in my candid fashion—he's a personable and intelligent young man— but she shrugged him off. I'm sure nothing is further from her mind than holy wedlock. Seems she has too much to do, see, and experience to settle for the usual— at least they were usual in my time—preoccupations."

"An admirable attitude, and one which I share."

"We'll see.... What have you been doing?"

"I've told you, Gran."

"Just that you've been hired as a jack-of-all-trades,

57

and apparently didn't have sense enough to ask what Westcott will pay you."

"I told you 'peanuts.' He told Nick Denton."

"Who's Denton?"

"Advertising manager. I also met Tom Williams, reporter, and Mary O'Malley, in charge of the woman's page."

"And your impressions?"

"Good."

"How about Mary O'Malley?"

"Thin, nervous, about fifty, friendly."

"Well," Vanessa decided, "you won't starve, whatever Si pays—thanks to your grandfather. On the other hand you won't amass an earned fortune."

Adam laughed. He said, "There's another co-worker, Carol Benson, assistant to Mrs. O'Malley. She writes feature stories for the woman's page. I met her Saturday night—with the Osbornes. She wasn't in the office today."

"She will be. In retrospect I've never, since your grandfather divorced me, been in as much danger as you have since, say, eighteen. Make that twenty-one. Men are hapless and helpless when confronted with predatory females. Of course, marriage has become rather prehistoric, but some women retain an unliberated determination.

"Adam, tomorrow after whatever work you do is concluded, come and walk with me to the stone wall. Bing came by this morning, I have his permission. Then, unless otherwise engaged, stay for early supper. I'll order, and supervise, and promise to dismiss you when

I tire—or Angie will, when she comes by."

"To hear is to obey." He kissed the top of his grandmother's untidy white head. "Be a good girl, Gran," he advised just as Edna came in. He had timed his departure to her appearance.

5

Suddenly on Tuesday the temperature and humidity were high and children frolicked in swimming pools of all sizes and shapes. Commuters cursed when the train pulled in bereft of its air conditioning. The office of the *Beacon* employed only fans, and Adam was as busy as a citizen of an ant hill. He took his orders from Nick Denton, who bestowed an advertising-rate card upon him, and then explained what agate line, flat rate per column, discounts, long-term contracts, and other mysteries meant.

"You'll soon memorize it all," he said kindly. "Just now your job is to sell your personality. Most of the time I just call up and get renewals. But here's a list of reluctant advertisers who feel they can't afford as much as last year. And here's another of new people who haven't quite made up their minds as to how much and how often. You might also look in on what we trust are satisfied customers just to say hello."

Carol Benson came in, smiled at Nick and Tom, remarked, "It's hot," and then caught sight of Adam. "Don't tell me," she implored him. "Let me guess. You're on staff."

"I empty trash baskets," he told her.

"Good. You might find something in them of value. It's recently been done on high levels.... Wait for me."

She vanished in the direction of the O'Malley office. Nick shook his head and Tom said, sighing, "Well, good luck."

Carol barreled back again, took Adam's arm, and suggested briskly, "Let's go.... Where to, for you?"

He told her and she said, "I wish you were a photographer; you could come with me. The guy we employ is off taking pictures of horses, wrecked cars, and two dumps. But I'm about to try to persuade two old ladies in a condominium to grant interviews."

"Abby Allen and Emily Warner?"

"I forgot you were Inner Circle."

"Why do you want stories of them?"

"Because Mrs. Allen has refused ever since she returned here to live in her parental home—and as a diplomat's widow she's good material. Mrs. Warner always has been, I suppose, but not until they sold their houses and bought in the Revolution Hill Villas complex was it worth a try. Do you really know them?"

"Slightly."

She flipped a hand. "I don't have an appointment, and they probably have guard—if not attack—dogs. I've never met Mrs. Allen, though I have met Mrs. Warner once. The O'Malley—as I refer to my boss—says I'm insane to even contemplate asking what it's like to be a diplomat's widow or a retired big-shot realtor." Carol looked at her watch. "I'm off to the battle," she added. "If you happen to be around the Checkered Tablecloth at, say twelve, you can hear all about it and have lunch at the same time."

Adam went his way and fulfilled his obligations; he stopped in shops where he was not known and introduced himself; he called on people he knew. In the bookshop there were three: Jeremy Palmer; his partner, Sam Peters; and Sam's wife, Sara, who had come in from giving a French lesson to look at some newly arrived foreign books that she had ordered. She still worked in the shop part-time.

Adam asked, "May I sit down? My feet, as they say, are killing me."

"Take off your shoes," Sara suggested.

"Thanks, no," he said with dignity and Sam asked, "What are you doing pounding the pavements? Police force?"

"Errand boy for the *Beacon*, where I'm to do odd jobs, very odd, keep an eye on old clients, and sell a little more advertising."

"Don't turn your charm on me," Sam advised. Just tell Nick I'll talk to him before the carols start."

"Speaking of carols," Adam said, "do any of you know Carol Benson?"

None knew her but all had seen her. "She's not," said Sam sadly, "the literary type."

"Well, in a way. She writes feature articles for the woman's page. No byline yet, but she's new here. She

62

lives with the Westcotts. Si's her aunt's husband," Adam said.

"So far," Sam said, "I've just seen her around." Sara added, "She came in once for a French dictionary," and Sam admitted, "I noticed."

Adam laughed and said to Sara, "At this moment, more or less, she is up at Revolution Hill trying to coax interviews from your grandmother and Mrs. Warner."

"*Herr Gott!* The girl will come home on her shield," Sara predicted.

"It ain't necessarily so," said her husband.

"Why?" Sara demanded.

"The last time we had dinner with your grandmother, which was probably ten days ago, she said she was thinking of writing her memoirs. She'd borrowed a number of autobiographies from the lending library, all by women—ladies of stage, screen, or title."

"She'll never do it," Sara said firmly.

"Don't be too sure. However, Emily won't cooperate."

"Why not?" asked Adam.

"For all those years Emily worked her tail off, as she often said—once, I recall, at a Chamber of Commerce dinner. But when she retired, she retired," Sam reported. "She has no interest in publicity. Her only professional contact is, of course, with her successor, our own Katie. Emily and Sara's grandmother now live the good, unhurried life. They consult one or the other of the Doctors Irvington regularly. They read, watch television, see movies, take short trips, walk, listen to music, occasionally go to the city. They have a delightful town house, a small garden that Emily tends, and a

63

middle-aged housekeeper. Last year the big decision was whether to buy a household pet or not. Emily likes cats, Abby hates them. Abby wanted a toy poodle. In the end, they compromised and bought goldfish."

Adam rose. "I must trudge on," he told them.

"How about coffee?" Sara asked.

"Thanks, no. I have a sort of lunch date." He looked at his watch and said, "One more stop, then it's ham on rye."

"Wait a minute. How's Vanessa?" Jeremy asked.

"Undaunted," Adam answered. "I'll tell her you asked."

"Tell her Katie and I will come see her," Jeremy said.

"Okay." He waved and departed and Sara said, "I wonder if he's fallen for Carol Benson."

"Women!" her husband said indulgently. "Adam mentions the girl once and you leap to the usual conclusion."

"He had a sort of anticipatory look in his eye," Sara explained, "as if he'd just opened a book and didn't know what it was about, much less know the ending."

"We should have a branch of special agents, all female—the intuitive squad," Sam said.

Adam turned up at the coffee shop where several people were at the small tables with the red-and-white-checkered cloths, but Carol was not among them. He found a wall table, ordered coffee, and said he was waiting for a friend. He was halfway through the cup when Carol came in, flushed and pretty.

"I'm sorry," she said, sitting down opposite him, just as the young waitress came up. "I'll have a B.L.T., but no mayonnaise, salt and pepper, and the bread sliced thin, and black coffee," Carol ordered.

The girl nodded, and asked Adam, "And you, sir?"

"Ham on rye," he said. "Mustard, and more coffee, please."

He smiled and she trotted off, dazzled. Carol watched her go. "You have an interesting effect upon females—or so I judge," she said.

"You've experienced it personally?" he asked hopefully.

"No. I've never been overwhelmed by charm; in fact I'm allergic to it. My former husband was permeated with charisma. What would personally interest me, given time, would be your background and your mind —I've assumed you have one—"

"Not my personality?"

"No."

"Why my background?"

The sandwiches came and Carol nibbled hers thoughtfully. Adam noted she had a firm grip on a usually rather sloppy situation. She answered presently, "I'm always interested in people with solidly solvent backgrounds, who grew up with security."

"My mother destroyed my blanket," Adam said sadly.

"I mean it," Carol insisted. "Growing up was a struggle for me. I worked my way through college. I got a job without using influence. Granted, the present one is due to Uncle Si, but I'm worth the pittance and I'll go on from here."

"Tell me about your interviews," Adam said.

"Mrs. Allen was pleasant. It's remarkable," said Carol

with valid astonishment, "that a woman her age can be so beautiful. Mrs. Warner, however, said that she couldn't tell me anything more than I already knew, which is that for a great many years she had successfully conducted a real estate business. By the way, Mrs. Allen asked me if I had interviewed your grandmother. When I said no, but I hoped to, she laughed. What does that mean?"

"I haven't the slightest idea," said Adam truthfully. "Anyway you're not going to—"

"Why not? From the bits and pieces I've heard, she's by far the most interesting character in Little Oxford, and according to Mrs. Allen—"

Adam scowled and Carol said hastily, "You needn't turn savage. All I do in these little harmless interviews is my job."

"My grandmother," Adam told her, "is not a character. She's a person *with* character, which is something else. She's been very ill, as you know, and she, far more than Mrs. Warner, is averse to publicity even in a small-town paper. She's a private woman, has only a few close friends—Mrs. Allen isn't one of them—and that's it. Sorry."

"No. you're not."

"That's right." He smiled, erasing the frown. "Are you busy Saturday?" he asked.

"I should say yes or that I'll have to check. But Saturday is boring.... No, I'm not. Make me an offer."

"I thought I'd call Mrs. Niles's caretaker, Jim, and inquire if we can use the pool,—if you wish, in the morning, and then go to lunch—or in the afternoon, and then have dinner."

"I'll settle for dinner. Does Mrs. Niles allow bikinis?"

"She would if she were here. She's in Europe with one of her protégées who, she hopes, will become another Beverly Sills.... Okay," he added, and beckoned for the check. "You can tell me Friday when to call for you. Are you going back to the office now?"

"No, don't hurry me. Pay that hovering girl and get going. I'll finish my coffee and read over my notes."

To her amazement, he obeyed.

The notes weren't very exciting. It would be gratifying, she thought, to do one of her interviews with a woman who wasn't quite a lady, or a man who wasn't all business and local enthusiasm.

Abby Allen had talked of her travels in the long years as a diplomat's wife and of her granddaughter.

Dull, thought Carol. No duels or lovers. Well, who'd expect that anyway? She'd do a harmless little piece on graciousness and beauty. Mrs. Allen had, alas no "suitable" photographs and had gently declined to see the press photographer.

Carol departed for the office, with her notebook thinking of Saturday and wondering about Mrs. William Niles. She had seen the elegant modern house, and caught a glimpse of the pool. She had heard of Mrs. Niles's great interest in young singers. Too bad, she thought, that I can't sing. Now, if it were acting... She'd done a spot of that in high school and college and rather fancied herself. There was an enthusiastic amateur group in Little Oxford and her aunt had urged her to try out. So far she hadn't. She also knew that Mrs. Niles had been born in Little Oxford, had married an orchestra leader, and sung in nightclubs. There wasn't much percentage in thinking she'd be a good local subject since, from what Carol had heard, everyone knew everything about her already. If what she discovered were less than devout, so to speak—which she'd also heard was the case—neither her uncle nor the O'Malley would print it. The only area in which criticism was permitted was on the editorial page, relative to town or outside politics, and in letters to the editor on diverse local controversies.

Adam, having concluded his rounds and reporting to Nick, had gone out with Williams to view what remained of a new house following a mysterious fire. At something after five he stopped at Vanessa's and found her in consultation with Edna in the kitchen.

"About time," said Vanessa, more briskly than she felt. "Let's go."

She dreaded the walk across the field to the wall and the little mound, on which grass now grew, and the triangle of small stones.

She looked down, then away. "He might have waited," she said and Adam, who knew better than to put his arm around her at this moment, said gravely, "He had no choice, Gran."

"Damned ambulance," she said. "If they'd taken me in an ordinary car, he wouldn't have panicked."

Adam heard the step before she did. It was Angie, looking tanned and windblown; she had a small cluster of flowers in her hand, and said, "I didn't know you'd be here, Mrs. Steele."

"Well, I am," Vanessa assured her. She looked at Angie, obviously hesitant, and said brusquely, "All right, put them down, but come back and pick them up before they're wilted. I can't stand wilted flowers. Come back with us to the house, there's enough for supper."

Angie, walking beside her, did not offer to steady her as Adam had put his grandmother's hand on his arm. But she watched, marking the slow deliberate steps, the slight wavering.

"I'm sorry, I can't," she said. "I have to help my mother."

"A glass of wine," Vanessa insisted, "won't take long."

So Angie stayed for a glass of white wine and cheese and crackers, and as she left Vanessa said, "Thanks, Angie."

Adam went to the door with her. She looked at him and smiled. "Don't worry so much," she advised. "She's better, honestly she is. Her stamina and will power—they're remarkable. It will take time. She'll never be exactly as she was before her illness—and she's impatient, which doesn't help—but she's gaining."

"You're a tremendous help," Adam said. "Incidentally, the last time my father was here he said if anything ever happened to him he'd send for you. He's hooked on competence and tranquility, which both my parents lack. Me too. He's also hooked on pretty girls."

"I'm flattered," said Angie, who wasn't. She knew she was competent, unflappable, and pretty. She saw herself in the mirror daily and also in the eyes of many young, middle-aged, and old men. She had been born serene, she'd learned competence, and she had grown up almost beautiful, but she took credit only for study, application, and hard work. Her sole surrender to anxiety was her father's disability and her mother's constant, if rarely displayed, despair. Her only regret was that she had not become, as she'd wished, a registered nurse, but she consoled herself by thinking there'd still be time when she was no longer needed on the farm. She could start all over again.

Angie went on home. She was going out that night with Jack Wright—first a movie, than a drive. For some time she'd been troubled about him. Their association had been fun and lighthearted, but recently he had become serious, hence a problem. She did not want to marry him—or anybody else.

Vanessa said to Adam during supper, "You saw your redhead today."

"And you've been at the crystal ball again."

"She's in the office, isn't she?"

"Well, yes; I took her to lunch after her interviews with Mrs. Allen and Mrs. Warner."

"Interviews?"

"I told you Carol writes stately little society-page pieces about local celebrities. She'd like to do you."

"We do not grant interviews," Vanessa said at her most stately, and laughed. "And what," she asked, "did your co-worker get out of it? From Mrs. Allen, I mean. Emily wouldn't be bothered."

"Oh, I gather just a short recital of her travels. Incidentally, Mrs. Allen asked if Carol had been to see you."

"Why?"

"I've no idea, except she thinks you're a character."

To his astonishment Vanessa flushed, and then said, "Damned impertinent of her."

Saturday afternoon, on his way to pick up Carol, Adam was thinking of Vanessa. She seemed, during the last few days, to have regained something of her old vigor, if sometimes only for a few minutes. He saw her every day unless he was out of town dutifully submitting to his mother's sighs and his father's irritability. So far no really interesting weekends, however. One couldn't count Toby.

Vanessa had said, "I must admit I feel better. Perhaps because everyone tries so hard to make me so. I'm in constant contact with what I can only characterize as good thoughts—which sometimes infuriates me. On the medical end, there's Bing and Ben and, of course, Angie, who has a natural talent with invalids, for which her father must be grateful. Edna too in her way, and Stacy, Lee, and the Palmers." She'd smiled then. "All the young people—anyone under fifty is young—including you, Adam."

Si Westcott's house was on a quiet street, tree-shaded, and on about two acres. He owned other acreage that he was holding against further depressions and inflations, and other houses that he rented. He'd been born in this house, as had his father and grandfather.

Carol was on the front porch, carrying what looked like a flight bag. She said, "You're late."

"Sorry about that; stopped at Gran's. Hop in."

She hopped, remarking, "This car must be nearly as old as your grandmother."

"If it were, I'd sell it and retire. Don't denigrate any mode of locomotion.... I rather like my willful vehicle, but I miss my motorcycle."

Carol shrugged. "Dreadful noisy things," she said and added, "I forgot to ask, is there a place to change at your Mrs. Niles's?"

"Several, and the car isn't mine. I wish she were. I've always liked older women. I keep telling them so."

Later, he said, "We turn off here. You'll meet Jim Preston, on arrival."

"Who's he?"

"The caretaker. Lives over the garage. The housekeeper, Addie, just comes in to clean, though she lives in when Mrs. Niles is home. They're all natives."

"Like Mrs. Niles?"

"Yes, of course. If you've been asking about her, you already know that. And so is your uncle and his ancestors; also Abby Allen. Emily Warner's husband was born here, but she came from a town just across the state line. I suppose you know the Comstocks?"

"By sight—the younger ones."

"Well, Matt's father's housekeeper is Jim Preston's cousin by marriage. I've never asked Matt how many generations his people have been here—as many as Letty Irvington's perhaps."

"I understand from Aunt Edie that it took some time for her to creep into the charmed circle, as she was born upstate. It's ridiculous. Me, I like a big city—lots of people, mostly strangers, and no one trying to climb your family tree to see what's hanging from it."

"Oh well, cheer up," he said. "The population explosion hit Little Oxford some time ago so there will be a hell of a lot more natives in twenty years.... Here we are."

He got out, opened her door, lent her a hand, and shouted, "Jim!"

Jim appeared, tan and broad-shouldered and gave her a direct blue gaze. "This is Carol Benson," said Adam. "She's Si Westcott's niece."

"Wife's," Jim corrected. "Nice woman, Edie... Hi, Carol."

What a town, Carol thought, following Jim and Adam, where you were presented to the caretaker—along with your credentials.

The house was big, contemporary, glass, with sun decks and a patio surrounding the pool.

"Man came," said Jim. "Sometimes when Mrs. Niles is away I have to remind him. It's clean as a whistle. I put up the umbrellas every day. Now and then the Palmers come, and the Osbornes—Matt and Maggie too. It's the best pool in town and, if I say so as I shouldn't, the best kept. You know your way around, Adam."

"Some. Wait, I forgot. I brought you some Westerns, they're on the back seat."

"Thanks, it'll be a change. Jeremy lent me a couple of books last week, *The Widow of Windsor* for one, *The War of the Roses* for another. Have a good swim," Jim said.

He went off toward the car and Carol asked, "What was that all about?"

"He's a reader, and has Catholic tastes, history, biography, Westerns, mysteries, and gothics."

Adam led the way to the wing of the house. "Guests," he explained. "There are two dressing rooms for bathers." He added, "I'll be next door," and vanished, carrying his trunks and a towel.

When they reconvened at pool's edge, Carol asked, "Is it heated?"

"No. It's cooler than a fiord—artesian wells. However, it's had considerable sun lately. There are steps," he added, "for the timid. Last one in is a shrinking violet."

She watched him dive, admiring the lean muscular body. She did not want to dive, but neither did she wish to lower herself by inches into what could be iced water. So she dove, and came up gasping. Eventually they sat poolside and admired each other. Carol's bikini was emerald green—what there was of it.

"Hand me that towel. I'm freezing," she said.

The towel was also green. She took off her cap and the auburn hair streamed down.

"You and your fiord!" she said.

"Pull yourself together. I'll race you presently. Loser gets sympathy and a kiss. All my girls lose and love it," he said complacently.

Carol lost and he kissed her soundly right there in the pool. Jim passing by—after all, you have to keep an eye on things—shook his head. He knew a little about Carol Benson. His late wife's cousin, Bert, did odd jobs for the Westcotts.

"Tired?" Adam asked.

"A little. But it's been fun. I find it easy to envy Mrs. Niles."

"Money? Don't. She has problems too. Once you really know someone, you can't envy them."

"Don't you envy anyone?"

"No. Just talent. Rosie Niles's talent for helping young musicians and for making her own life more tolerable. Stacy Osborne's art, which kept her going until she met Lee; Lee's gift as an architect; Jeremy Palmer's two beautiful obsessions—his family and books. The Irvingtons' dedication to medicine and to others. I have no talent," he told her, "unless it's for living. I daresay I inherited that from my grandmother."

"She's a native, isn't she?"

"No. But she's lived here a long time and as she never asked or cared to be accepted, she has been. You have a very large streak of curiosity, Carol."

"I'm a journalist."

"There are no 'journalists' on the *Beacon*, just reporters. What's your goal—a byline column in a city newspaper or a TV talk show?"

"My aspirations," she told him, flicking a slender foot in the pool, disturbing the reflection of the summer sky, "don't include hard work or clawing my way up an unsteady ladder—just being where I can meet, and entrap, a rich man."

"You astound me."

"No, I don't; you're not stupid. Anyway, I'd like the opportunity. I've had the opposite side of the coin—a poor man, romantic, charming, and a loser."

He said, "But you were in love with him."

"Of course, as much as I could be with anyone—but it wore off." She looked into the water and shivered. "I'm cold," she said.

A small breeze ruffled the pool and Adam said, helping her up, "Okay. We'll get dressed and I'll take you back to my burrow, and then we'll go to dinner."

In the car Carol said, "I didn't ask what *your* ambition is—if you have any."

"Of course. I can't be what I'd like to be, which is a musician, but I'd like to own a newspaper one day, in a small town—like this one."

"You're nuts," Carol told him. "Look at Uncle Si."

"I've looked. I like what I see, a solid, solvent man who inherited a good thing and made it better. He has a pleasant house, a delightful wife, and a pretty, if mercenary, niece by marriage."

"Thanks a lot."

"You're welcome," he told her. And then, "just around the corner, my modest hovel."

Carol, going in, looked around. "It's attractive," she said, "it's the Osbornes', isn't it?"

"Yes."

"I interviewed them in their house next door."

"It's coming down," Adam told her, "and there'll be new houses. This place will be all sound and fury before long, so take advantage of the present peace and quiet.... May I fix you a drink?"

"I don't drink except, at dinner, a glass of wine."

"Unusual and commendable," he told her.

"No, just calculating. Shouldn't you take me home so I can change?"

"We aren't going where it's necessary...just to a new place out toward the lake. You can go there in jeans if you prefer, in anything but bathing suits—or bikinis—or barefoot. It opened a couple of weeks ago, and may bring some competition to the Greek restaurant—not much, as its run *by* young people *for* young people. They have good inexpensive food and a jukebox."

"Sounds horrible."

"Don't be apprehensive," Adam said. "I can't live on my salary, but now and then I try. Like tonight."

"You picked the wrong time."

"Just testing. Maybe during the summer, if we're still friends, I'll treat you to dinner at Chez Nous or the Inn and, of course, the Aegean. Not tonight, Your Majesty. I'm mixing business with—I'm almost sure—pleasure. I hope Larry and Gwen will think about a small advertisement. Forget your fantasies of caviar and pheasant. Brush your beautiful hair, powder your snub nose, lay on the lipstick. There's a guest convenience off the second bedroom. Don't be too long, I'm hungry."

Looking into the mirror and, as usual, liking what she saw, she thought: It's just my luck that he isn't loaded. Then she remembered that, barring sudden irreparable misfortune, he would be someday. But someday was far distant and she hadn't time to wait.

The New Place was called just that—a modest sturdy building, with a good parking lot and trees clustered around in the back. There were scrubbed tables, paper table mats, stoneware, thick glasses. It was fairly full, and a plain young woman came up and said, "Hi, Adam."

He said, "Hello, Gwen, you have a table?" and she told him with an irradiating smile, "More than one, I'm sorry to say."

She looked at Carol in the way most women did, with inquiry and envy; Adam made the introductions, and Gwen took them to a table for two not too near the jukebox, which was playing Elton John.

The menu was on a slate: hamburgers, fried chicken, steak sandwiches, and salads.

"Can you afford the steak?" Carol inquired politely.

"Yes, since it isn't filet mignon. Try the homemade soup. It's excellent. You'll get French fries, homemade bread, and a salad," he promised, "and coffee. Dessert's extra, but I can manage. It's ice cream or home-baked cake."

Larry arrived, and Adam gave the order. "Steak," he said, "rare, for us both—or isn't it?" he asked Carol.

Carol, who liked her steak rare, said perversely, "It's chancier than medium."

"Rare," said Adam firmly.

When Larry had departed, Carol said, "Isn't it odd how handsome men often marry plain wives?"

"Some just don't want competition, but Gwen isn't plain," Adam told her. "She's a very unusual girl, completely herself. And Larry isn't handsome, he simply gives that impression."

Before they left, Adam excused himself and left Carol to contemplate youngsters in jeans and T shirts, eating or dancing, feeding the hungry jukebox and themselves. When Adam returned, Carol asked, "Well, did you sell a little advertising?"

"A small order, starting the July Fourth weekend—business is good and it will get better, Larry thinks—two column inches, ten insertions, but you wouldn't know about that."

"Certainly I know. Congratulations."

Gwen came to the door with them and Carol thought: He's right, she isn't exactly plain. In the car she said to Adam, "I don't understand why she isn't plain—nondescript features, ordinary coloring, nothing hair, average figure—so why isn't she plain?"

"Because," said Adam, "she's happy.... Shall we stop at the studio? I can offer you a glass of good wine as a nightcap."

"Not this time, maybe the next." She pondered briefly and then asked, "How about Wednesday?"

"Fine, but remember, I'm not eligible," he told her, standing on the Westcott doorstep.

"I never said I'd give up amusing myself. Thanks and good night."

80

Adam drove home, wondering if it was too late to call Vanessa. Just as he arrived, Edna called him. She said, "I tried before, no answer—"

"I'm sorry. Is anything wrong?"

"No. Mrs. Steele is fine and wants to speak to you."

When Vanessa took over the wire, she demanded, "Where have you been?"

Adam chuckled. "Your normal baritone sounds querulous. Out, Granny, with an interesting kitten."

"The red-and-white ones are always female," remarked Vanessa, "and are called money cats.... Your father telephoned. Your mother has a sort of summer flu. He tried the studio. No answer, so he called me with his usual mixture of terror and respect."

"I've a dinner date with Stacy and Lee tomorrow to talk over the big move, but I can get to the parents and back in time; coming or going, I'll stop by to see you."

"Not to worry." Vanessa thought of her daughter-in-law, Emily, and shook her head. "Your mother will recover once six doctors persuade her that the diet she's been on for years is slowly killing her. She looks like a splinter. Forget me. I'll survive not seeing you tomorrow."

"No, you won't, and I'd hate to feel guilty."

"I'm sure it would be a rare experience. Give Stacy and Lee my love. Tell her not to move furniture or lift cartons."

"Lee won't let her lift a paper napkin."

"I feel very smug about that marriage," Vanessa said. "If it hadn't been for me, Stacy wouldn't have met Lee Osborne."

81

"Don't be too sure," Adam advised her. "On the other hand if it hadn't been for you, I wouldn't have been born."

"You have unsmugged me," said Vanessa and hung up. She looked at Edna and smiled. "Men," she said. "Get thee to a convent."

Edna looked startled. "But I'm not a Roman Catholic," she argued, astonished, and thought: It's good to hear her joke that way again.

Calling for Carol on Wednesday evening Adam apologized for his car. "Sorry, it isn't a Ferrari," he told her. "The car parker at Chez Nous will probably put it somewhere obscure so a Cad—no pun intended—can run into, or over, it."

"I'm sure you can afford something a little more recent," Carol told him.

"Naturally. But cars, like ships, are women. I told you I like older women."

Arriving at the restaurant in the small community of Saltmarsh, Adam looked with amusement at the ill-concealed disdain upon the acne-scarred face of the youth who suggested, "Take your car, sir?" and to whom he handed a folded bill. "Take care of her," he said gently. "Someday she'll be an antique."

As he had a reservation, they were escorted with some show of interest to a good table. The menu came, followed by the wine steward. Adam said genially to his guest, "Gorge yourself, but no caviar. I have bought caviar only for Shadow."

"Shadow?"

"My grandmother's cat."

"Oh, yes. I'd heard about him but forgotten."

"He tolerated only young men, but no boys, one dog, people who understood him, and pretty girls.

As they were leaving, Adam looked across the room. "There's Angie," he said and touched Carol's bare, tanned arm. "Let's say hello."

Angie was with an attractive male at a table for two, and when they reached it, Adam said, "Hi, Angie. What are you doing out?"

"For good behavior," Angie told him, "I have the night off." She looked from him to Carol and he made the introductions as did she; her companion was Dr. John Wright.

"Who's she?" asked Carol when the attendant had tenderly delivered Adam's car.

"Angie Barker. Her people own a farm. She's an LPN. She lives at home taking care of her father who has been very ill. She also looks in on Gran every day."

"Earth-woman type?"

"You don't fancy it?"

"Women with no makeup except lipstick, fine skin, clear candid eyes, and suffused by what is known as a natural glow, irritate me. I've known a few in my time. My former husband's preference, incidentally, after I ceased to attract him.... Who's Dr. Wright?"

"He's a resident at the hospital. Don't set traps. He's

not yet in private practice—and when he is, it will be light years before he can afford a wife or girl friend plus malpractice insurance.... Are we stopping at my place?"

"No, I prefer uncomplicated relationships as a rule."

"Okay."

At the Westcotts', Carol said, "I'd ask you in, but this is manicuring night. Thank you for dinner. See you around."

Going home Adam reflected that one of Carol's ploys was to play hard to get, but not always, he was certain, and not if a million dollars came around the corner with a sign reading, *Up for Grabs.*

Carol, in her pleasant bedroom at the Westcotts', after her manicure, hair brushing, and facial, lay in the four-poster, her arms behind her spectacular head. Since her aborted marriage to the improvident Mr. Benson, she had become a researcher. But in Little Oxford, no research had been necessary as far as her interviews were concerned; her subjects were candid, if sometimes reluctant, and what they didn't tell she could find out—and use—up to a point. Si would have set fire to his building rather than print gossip, rumor, or the slightest scandal. Let the daily national press do that. When a resident of Si's town got involved in a sensational lawsuit, or was caught with a hand in the till, it went unmentioned in his paper.

Carol's casual encounter with Angie Barker had made no impression besides convincing her that, earth woman or not, Angie would be very appealing to most men. Thinking of this now, she congratulated herself on always *being,* if not *playing,* fair. But Angie's escort interested her, so before going to her room and her manicuring set, she had looked for his name in the local telephone book. It was not there, unless, of course, he was a son of one of the several Wrights who lived in Little Oxford.

Maybe he lived in one of the hospital apartments, or perhaps he was from Deeport or somewhere in the area. There would have been a notice in the *Beacon* at the time he came to the hospital, only if Dr. Wright were a Little Oxfordian; hence no point in searching files.

She reflected that it was time to have lunch in the coffee shop at the hospital with Aunt Edie's friend and distant relative, Violet Marcy, who worked there part-time as a nurse. The last time Vi had come to the Westcotts' for supper, which was a couple of weeks ago, she'd invited Carol to the shop for a cup of coffee and a hamburger.

"I'll call her from the office," Carol decided.

She did so in between working and listening to the continuing saga of the O'Malley's too-fecund daughter-in-law. Mrs. Marcy said, sure she'd stop by the coffee shop at, say, noon Saturday. They were very busy on the floor, she explained, but she could take half an hour.

Vi Marcy was around forty and a graduate of the hospital. She had worked there before her marriage, and after her twin girls were in high school she had returned, working irregular days and hours. Her husband was employed by a contractor. "Someone had to

be home sometime," she'd said that night at the Westcotts'. "Bill's away a lot—building has begun again,
thank God, and the business has picked up. Between
us, however, we manage to keep two pairs of eyes on
the girls."

Over coffee on Saturday, Vi made small talk. The
twins, now sixteen, were at the age when phones ring
continually. Neither she nor Bill believed in going
steady at sixteen, so instead of just two boys calling for
dates, there were hordes.

It was ten minutes—and Vi kept looking at the wall
clock—before Carol asked, "What do you know about
Dr. Wright?" There was no time for finesse.

Vi's round serene face expressed mild astonishment.
"Why?" she asked.

"I met him briefly the other night. He was with a
girl named Barker."

"Angie. Everyone loves her," said Vi with enthusiasm.

"I'm sure of it," said Carol. "I was just wondering
if Dr. Wright is from Little Oxford or nearby."

"Oh, no. Long Island, I think. His father is Otis
Wright, with offices in the city. He's a very nice young
man. Jack, I mean—and popular with everyone."

On Monday, Carol asked her uncle, "Have you ever
heard of someone named Otis Wright?" and Si had
responded, "Sure, oil. Why?"

Carol fetched the office copy of *Who's Who*—a lot of
area people found their way into the wrist-breaking vol-
ume—and looked up Otis Wright. There were several,
but her quarry indeed had a home in Suffolk County;
in addition he had an apartment and office in the city;

a wife with a New Amsterdam maiden name; a son, Dr. John Wright; and two daughters, Mrs. Heron and Miss Lucy.

It was not difficult for Carol to enter the coffee shop alone, sit in a corner, looking at the clock, finally ordering, drinking the coffee, and departing. But it wasn't until the third time, sneaking off on her lunch hour, that she struck what is sometimes known as pay dirt.

"Hi," she said to Jack Wright, who was walking past her, also alone.

"Well, hi," he responded, with that who-are-you look, and then, "I remember—the other night at Chez Nous." He smiled down at her, a tall young man with brown hair that inclined to curl, and an easy manner. "I've forgotten your name. Forgive me."

He hadn't, however, forgotten her.

"I'm Carol Benson," she said. "I was with Adam Steele.... Are you waiting for someone?"

"No. Are you?"

"Well, I'd hoped to have lunch with Mrs. Marcy, but she's too busy."

"May I sit down?" He did so, saying, "We're all too busy." A volunteer came up and he said, "Hello. I'll have the usual."

Carol looked after her as she walked away. "Is that Stacy Osborne?" she asked.

"Yes...you don't know her? I'm sorry," said Jack. "I should have introduced you."

"I've seen her," Carol told him, "and she's a favorite

of Uncle Si's. I've looked at her paintings at the Gallery, interesting work," added Carol, who begrudged any talent.

"They're at the Gallery permanently I believe. Stacy gave them to Janice and Ed Reynolds after her first show."

"She's very attractive."

"Yes. Little Oxford has some spectacular beauties."

"Do you know the Steeles, Dr. Wright?"

"Slightly. A friend of mine looks in on Mrs. Steele, and has since her heart attack. I saw Mrs. Steele in the hospital. Remarkable woman. I met her grandson for the first time with you at Chez Nous."

"Your friend is Angie Barker? Oh, of course, she lives near Mrs. Steele," said Carol. "Such a pretty girl."

Stacy came with Jack's order, introductions were made, and when she'd left Jack said. "We'll miss her here."

"The Osbornes are moving?"

"Only from one Little Oxford house to another, but this is Mrs. Osborne's last week in the coffee shop. But I daresay she'll still work in the hospital for a while, as long as she doesn't have to carry heavy trays or push book carts."

The patter of little feet, Carol decided, smiling. She must tell Si and Aunt Edie, not that the O'Malley would announce a pregnancy in the social notes.

When Dr. Wright announced that he had to get back to work, Carol said, "I hope we'll see each other again." He nodded and agreed that he did too. She didn't put much credence in the courteous reply, but thought perhaps she'd suggest a double date to Adam.

When she did so that afternoon—she was working on the O'Malley files when Adam strolled in—he looked mildly astonished. "That would be next to *Mission Impossible*," he told her. "Angie's as busy as he is."

"Suppose you try? We might make it before the first snow."

"In whom are you interested?"

"Both, of course."

"Nuts," said Adam. "Are you planning a takeover?"

Carol looked shocked. She said, "Don't be absurd," and then, "Why not? A girl has to consider every opportunity," she told him and, shaking his head, he went out to call on the owner of the new boutique. He thought: You can't trust her, but you have to admire her chutzpa.

When Adam saw his grandmother that evening, he said, "I'll be irregular in attendance, though faithful. I'm going to help the Osbornes move, packing cartons and such. I offered to officiate at a tag sale, if, of course, they'd give me a percentage," he added, laughing, "but it seems they've engaged a professional."

"I hate to have them move away."

"It's just to the village," he reminded her, "and you'll see them often."

"No bicycles," she said sadly.

Angie came in, and Adam went into the living room. When she emerged from Vanessa's room he asked, "Do you like things like pop music, light opera, amateur plays, and school sports in season?"

"Of course."

"Part of my job," he told her, "is reporting these events. Can I persuade you to go with me when you have the time?"

She smiled, "I'd love to. I went to Little Oxford High and was in the cast of some of the shows. Perhaps sometime when my father is better and Mrs. Steele doesn't need me."

Summer stopped by with gifts of roses and rain, interruptions of heat and sun, then more rain. Carol remarked to the O'Malley that she wished the cold fronts would cease and desist. But Adam took torrents in his stride, as well as the sudden period of ninety degrees Fahrenheit.

Vanessa complained on days when she couldn't sit on the screened porch off the kitchen.

Fair or foul, the weather did not prevent people from trying to park where there was little space and lots of mud in order to listen to the groups and minstrels who came to the high school auditorium and the other public places; there were fireworks on the beaches and rock and roll in the parks, nostalgic, if loud. Angie managed two evenings with Adam, once in the rain, under a roof; the next time during uncommon humidity in the park. She enjoyed it and he thought he had never known a girl who liked crowds and musical noise, didn't mind where they sat, and never criticized. Carol, when he took her with him, always found something to worry at, like a dog with a bone—the music, the singers, costumes, the seats, the voices, the length of someone's hair, the selections.

"You," he said firmly on the last occasion, "are a born carper."

"I suppose so, and I shouldn't bitch," she admitted, "but—"

"Your tastes are more finely honed?" he suggested.

She shrugged. "There has to be an audience for any performer," she said. "I was born without talent so I learned to be an audience—an intelligent one."

"I concede," he said, and took her back to the Westcotts' and kissed her good night.

He wondered what Angie thought of him. She was cordial and serene always, often amusing. He told Vanessa once, "Angie's a strange girl. I think she likes me, but I'm not sure."

"She likes you," Vanessa said, "but I doubt she weeps on her pillow after you leave her. There's her medic."

"You said she had no idea of marrying him."

"Or anyone else, so rejoice. For the first time in your short life you have met a sensible girl who is a beauty."

One day, as summer pursued its primrose path, Carol Benson knocked on Vanessa's red door. She was demurely clad in a cool, abstract-print frock, she wore a becoming hat and carried gloves and a handbag. Her shoes were wedgies and her brown legs were bare. When Edna opened the door, Carol smiled and said apologetically, "I know Mrs. Steele isn't expecting me, but I've a message for her from her grandson."

Edna looked uncertain, opened her mouth to say that

she'd consult her employer, but Carol slid past her like a fish avoiding the hook, into the living room where Vanessa sat smoking one of her forbidden cigars. Looking up, she put it in an ashtray as Carol said, "Dear Mrs. Steele, forgive me. I'm Carol Benson, Si Westcott's niece. Adam had to take off for Deeport and asked me, since I was driving out this way, to tell you he'd be a little late this afternoon."

"Sit down," Vanessa barked in her undiminished baritone, "and let me look at you.... Yes, quite as I thought. However, I admire an unabashed liar. I know where Adam is. He is helping the Osbornes move and not to Deeport. I saw him last evening."

"Sorry," Carol told her, arranging herself in an adjacent chair, "but I simply had to meet you and Adam hasn't seen fit to bring me here."

Vanessa smiled slightly. She had met a good many Carols in her day.

"Naturally," she agreed. "I told him not to, as what you want is, I believe, a so-called interview."

"That's right. Just a little piece; I've written a number for the *Beacon* about our outstanding local residents."

"Perhaps you mean characters? I understand Mrs. Allen referred to me as one?"

"Of course," Carol agreed enthusiastically, "as you're such good friends—"

Vanessa uttered a short sharp word, one which Si wouldn't have printed. "I've encountered Mrs. Allen twice in my life," she said, "once at a party, once during a disaster. I don't give interviews. You may, therefore, return to your typewriter and report that you've seen

93

this house from the outside, this room; though I doubt that even in deathless prose it would cause a sensation. I've lived here a long time, I pay taxes, and contribute small amounts to causes I consider worthy. In addition, I am a practicing witch—and Si's is a conservative paper. In Little Oxford witches rev up their brooms only on Halloween.... Edna!"

Edna appeared and Vanessa said, "Please show Mrs. Benson out."

Carol remonstrated. "But Mrs. Steele—" she began.

"No," Vanessa said, "and be sure to cross yourself as you leave."

Carol rose, scarlet with—what? Rage? Humiliation?—and the impassive Edna escorted her to the door. Returning, she found Vanessa indulging in a spasm of belly laughter. When she had quieted, she said, "Don't ever let her in again—not that I think she'll try. However, she's capable of trying to bribe you or Angie or anyone on the block for information on my life and times."

"Whatever did she want?" asked Edna, bewildered.

"A little paragraph for the paper. Now she'll haunt the neighborhood looking for my demon lover."

"Good grief!" said Edna mildly.

8

Adam dropped by to drink a glass of wine and wolf
a few cheese puffs. He was going with Nick to a new
bistro, which had just opened near the *Beacon* and from
which Nick had secured advertising. The place was supposed to be good and inexpensive; it was called The
Whale and Minnow.

"Why give it such a name?" Vanessa asked.

"I daresay they serve both. Stacy, Lee, and Cora are
now moved into Emily's spotless house, which, of
course, Cora will reclean tomorrow. They didn't need
me except for moral support, so I managed to have
the afternoon off. When I left, Lee had put Stacy to
bed; everything was shipshape, the movers being an admirable crew; and Cora was whipping up a light supper
in the kitchen. That's a great house," said Adam, "new
as a Concorde, old as a surrey.... What have you been
up to?"

"Carol Benson.... You look peculiar when your jaw drops, Adam."

"She came *here?*"

"Yes," Edna confirmed. "In a small car."

Adam grinned. "I'm not surprised," he said.

"I was," said Vanessa. "*You* are astonished. Do mind your diction."

"I fear that she didn't get her interview. Really you should have unbent. I would have loved to have seen you with a *Widow of Windsor* face."

"I didn't wear it, On the contrary I *was* amused."

"She's just a poor working girl," Adam told her reproachfully.

"Of course. Incidentally, she lied through her capped teeth. She told Edna you had asked her to deliver a message."

"Very capable girl. I've assured her half a dozen times that you would never admit anything—especially to the press."

"Press, my left foot. But during your next meditation concentrate on the thought that she's written you off as a loss. Of course that's just an educated guess on my part."

"I know. Shortly after we met. Alas, no yachts in the family."

"Mrs. Benson has her hazel-green eye on Angie's personal physician."

"Who told you that?"

"Angie."

"But who told her?"

"Dr. Wright—unwittingly. He happened to mention

that he was passing through the hospital coffee shop when Mrs. Benson, alone at a table, hailed him; so they shared cakes and ale, or whatever was available at the time."

"But why?"

"My dear boy, have you never done intensive research on your chance-met friends. The good young doctor's father is heavily involved in a substance known as oil and in other financially satisfactory commodities. I was made privy to this by diverse young Florence Nightingales while recovering from my malady."

"I'll be damned!" exclaimed Adam.

"Probably," his grandmother conceded, "but you'll have fun along the way."

On the following morning Carol was in and out of the O'Malley office, but Adam caught up with her before noon and suggested, "If you haven't inspected our newest establishment, I'll meet you there at one. It's called The Whale and Minnow, and isn't Arthur Treacher's."

They met in the spotless dining room, the walls draped with fishnets, which had caught coral, shells, and starfish. Adam came early to talk to Joe and Pete, the two young men who owned it. He had been there for their opening; they had advertised the event and would continue to run small notices.

In the kitchen Joe, who cooked, directed his youthful staff of one, while Pete, who waited on tables, kept an eye on the dining room. "A good-looking chick," he announced. "Must be for you, Adam. So far no lone female has ventured in. Maybe only their husbands or boyfriends like fish. I'll whip out and tell her that, if it's vital, we also have hamburgers."

"Fine," Adam said. "I'm the bait here."

He strolled out and Carol said doubtfully, "I don't very much like fish."

"At ease," Pete told her, appearing suddenly. "We also serve mangled sirloin."

When they had settled on fish chowder for Adam, a cheeseburger for Carol, and coffee Adam said, "You look very pretty, Mrs. B. By the way, you're paying your own tab."

"How come?"

"You earn a living and can afford it. Besides, I'm angry with you."

Carol smiled, "I can see that. Is it anything unusual?"

"You had a hell of a nerve," he told her, "walking into my grandmother's den."

"Little Red Riding Hood," she admitted. "Well, actually there seemed no other way to get there."

"Also you lied. My grandmother admires liars. I do not."

"I had to say something," Carol told him pitifully.

"Well," said Adam, addressing himself to the excellent chowder and pilot biscuits, "you did say something, but you got nothing."

"I'm not so sure."

"What does that mean?"

"Are Mrs. Steele and Mrs. Allen feuding?"

Adam looked, and was astonished. He said, "As far as I know, they've met only twice. It would have had to have been a mammoth argument or a physical assault to provoke a feud. As it happens, I was present at their second meeting and no one went home in an ambulance or even in a snit."

"Mrs. Steele told me they'd met during a disaster."

"Ice storm," said Adam. "A group of people went to one of the few homes in the area that had a generator. Really, Carol, you should be writing gothics."

"Mrs. Allen, when I saw her, spoke of your grandmother as a 'character.' That's down-putting."

"I think you told me that. You don't belong here, Carol, nepotism or not. You should have a gossip column on a newspaper in a city, or appear beautifully garbed on TV, conveying wars, rumors of wars, and innuendos."

"I'm fond of you too," Carol told him sweetly.

Adam beckoned Pete. "Two checks," he said, and after Pete had complied, Adam added "Thanks," paid, and stalked out.

Pete looked after him and said, "You sure bugged him, Miss—"

"Carol Benson...Mrs.... Oh, he's just annoyed with me; he'll recover. May I have some hot coffee? Adam and I are both on the *Beacon*, you know. Tell me, where do you and your partner come from?"

All's grist...she thought. Joe and Pete might do for a piece on Little Oxford's opportunities for newcomers.

Having conquered Pete, Carol had her second cup of good coffee, gratis, and went her thoughtful way. There had to be something to the Steele–Allen situation; at least there had to be a situation. Adam was impossible, but she would ask around....

That night in her bedroom at the Westcotts'—having failed to manage a date with anyone—she deplored her incarceration in a provincial town, her inability to encounter Dr. Wright short of breaking a leg, and she told herself that if she never saw Adam Steele again, it would be years too soon. But she'd see him every day at work and sometimes on weekends, she knew, since she was more attracted to him than she'd been to anyone for a very long time. But if she let herself fall even half an inch in love with him, she'd cut her throat—or his.

Which, of course, brought her back to the Emergency Room, though she didn't fancy so dramatic an entrance.

Before she slept she thought: I may not be clairvoyant, but there's something definitely cockeyed between those two old women. Finding out what, could be entertaining and a source of delicate blackmail, which might open doors to houses she'd never entered.

Adam, taking his grandmother for her now daily early evening stroll to the stone wall, said, "Carol thinks you and Mrs. Allen have something going."

Vanessa stopped abruptly and braced herself on her cane, removing her hand from his arm.

"Such as what?" she inquired. "We're a little elderly, aren't we? Besides I've never been interested in the female of the species."

"Listen to her," said Adam to the stone wall. "Carol merely suggested a feud. Perhaps she meant rivalry," he added thoughtfully.

"If any, a very old one, and, as they say, in another

country, though neither wench is dead.... Back to the house; it's time for a glass of something. Your Carol reminds me of a silverfish, chomping its way through ancient histories."

"So there is something in it?"

As they started back across the summer fields Vanessa said, "Young women, old women, and most people of whatever sex talk too much. Abby Allen makes a some-what disparaging remark about me, I say I met her once—during a disaster—and Mrs. Benson puts two and two together and comes up with three hundred and forty-five on her personal computer. Of course there's something to it," she added crossly, "but it hardly concerns Little Miss Sherlock or, for that matter, you."

"Okay," said Adam. "Don't take on."

In the house Vanessa continued indignantly, "I wasn't taking on. Go help Edna with the tray."

He did so and then Vanessa commanded, "Sit down. I'd rather you didn't fret yourself into a delirium of curiosity. Once, prehistorically, I met Abby Allen's husband. She wasn't around at the time. That's it. Later she discovered that he had given me a small, valuable gift."

"How?"

"The way wives always discover things; she found a bill."

"Holy herring!" said Adam. "Where is it?"

"Where's what?"

"The evidence."

"I gave it away."

"To whom?" asked Adam.

"Stacy.... Drink your wine and go on home. I'm tired. I'll rest before supper."

Adam went his way, pondering. He knew something of Vanessa's erratic life and times, for she had given him glimpses of it—sometimes in reply to questions, sometimes speaking idly as from another existence. His mother, who knew very little about the senior Mrs. Steele, had often indulged in fantasies about her, since she disliked her mother-in-law very much. His father, on the other hand, usually rose in Vanessa's defense, though why, Adam had never understood, since she treated him as if he weren't a full pack. "Well, it's none of my business," Adam told himself, "and it's certainly not Carol's."

Summer drifted past, somnolent, burned by the sun, washed by the rain, noisy with thunder, brilliant with lightning. Little Oxford suffered the usual summer complaints; struck houses, struck trees, transformers. The older Irvingtons flew to California in July and returned, surfeited with rest, grandchildren, and parties. Ben and Amy Irvington, leaving Benjy with his grandparents, took off on their long-anticipated cruise. They came home brown, relaxed, danced out, and through—for the time being anyway—with frozen daiquiris and other rum potions, shopping, sightseeing, and people who asked at dinner tables, in the cocktail lounges, or at the pool, "And what is your specialty, Dr. Irvington?" once discovering that he was neither a PhD nor a clergyman.

Their small Benjy was as glad to see them as were his grandparents. "Somehow," said Letty to her husband, "I never dreamed that adorable baby would grow up to slam vacuum cleaners around, and, if turned loose, cause everything not nailed down to self-destruct in three minutes. I'm worn out."

"You'll live," said Bing. "You had a vacation before Benjy descended upon us. Anyway, he'll miss Oscar."

"He's a bad influence," Letty said darkly. "Oscar went right back to puppyhood once he realized Benjy was to live here a while, not just visit."

"I hope," said Bing, "that our only son will feel I've taken proper care of his practice."

"You loved it, particularly the charming women with allergies and Ben's summer-theater patients and the home-from- or going-to-college kids."

"You're absolutely right, as usual."

Letty came over to his chair and laid her silver-gilt, curly head against his, which was silver and copper. She said, "Well, neither Amy nor I seem to mind the kindly-old-doctor type, I suppose. How's Stacy?" she asked. "We must have the Osbornes over."

"She's fine. She has a long way to go yet and I think she'll enjoy every minute of it. Lee, she told me recently, is having strike trouble, so the tearing down of the Osborne house will be delayed. Vanessa growls every time the men turn up for work, but Adam, on the contrary, doesn't seem to mind."

He didn't. When the work was going on, they began early, but he soon left for work, and by the time he came home, they were gone. But his grandmother commented fretfully, "That house has been here longer than I have."

Adam said consolingly, "Maybe, when the new ones are built, interesting strangers will move in, like a quiet Jack the Ripper, or a thrifty old-fashioned madam from the West and I'll take you to call—I'll even drive you—and you can extract every last drop of information from them in your brutal little way…like, 'Was it fun cutting up the girls?' or, 'What sort of clientele did you have?' "

"You," said his grandmother, "are an idiot," and added as Angie came in, "isn't he?" Then, "If between us Edna and I can find something nourishing in these blasted times, why don't you both stay for supper?… Angie, can you get off?"

Angie could. She took Vanessa away for her injection and said firmly, "Rest for a little."

She and Adam walked up to the farm. Mr. Barker—looking well, and soon, he insisted, to be released from the damned wheelchair and walker—greeted them with enthusiasm. Sitting around drove him nuts; he'd started a stamp collection, he told Adam. Mrs. Barker, her serene face shining, asked, "How about supper?" but Angie said, "I've promised Mrs. Steele." The younger girls were home, so the senior Barkers would be all right and, before returning to Vanessa's, Angie walked Adam through the orchard. "Going to be a good crop," she said.

He looked at her with respect; she worked very hard, he thought and told her so. Angie laughed. "I like it. I'm sorry not to be on regular duty at the hospital—I'm on call if they really need me; I used to have quite a lot to do, and loved it. But I couldn't leave my mother alone when Pop was first ill, and the girls were at school."

"You don't get out enough."

"Oh, I do. Thanks to you and the music evenings and the ball games."

A sudden cold wind came up and shortly after they were back at Vanessa's it was raining, pouring down every which way the wind took it. Adam closed the windows and fastened the blinds and they had their pleasant supper by the first hearth fire of the season. It had turned raw and bone-piercing, and while they were drinking coffee in the living room Vanessa remarked, "If this keeps up I'll have to push up the thermostat. I've never minded changes in temperatures until the last few years; hot or cold, I adjusted like, I suppose, any healthy animal."

It was Angie who heard—through wind, rain, and the rattling of shutters—a crying at the door and a scratching sound. She had just said that, when there was a lull in the rain and wind, she must go home. Now she came to her feet saying, "Something's at the door."

"It isn't Halloween," Vanessa reminded her.

As Angie opened the red door, the rain blew in, the wind complained, and a sodden cat, shaking water from its paws and its coat, stalked into the living room, and sat down wetly on the hearth.

"Put it out," and "Poor thing," said Vanessa and Angie simultaneously.

The cat regarded them indifferently with large golden eyes, and Angie said, "I'll get an old towel." She made for the kitchen, adding over her shoulder, "and some milk."

"She's used to all kinds of creatures," Vanessa said, "but stray cats, once fed, are difficult to dislodge."

Angie returned with a saucer of milk and the towel. She set the saucer down, knelt by the vagabond in the firelight, and began to blot up the moisture. The cat did not move, even toward the saucer; it just sat there, with a certain complacent arrogance.

Adam was laughing. "A drop of brandy in the milk," he suggested, "otherwise it'll get pneumonia," and proceeded to spike the handout.

Vanessa swore in her uninhibited fashion. She said, "Now we'll never get rid of him."

Angie said, "It's all right, Mrs. Steele. I'll borrow a basket and take him back to the farm."

"To encounter your barn cats and your father's savage dog?"

"He'll get used to them—if he *is* a he—" Angie said calmly, "providing he wants board and lodging."

The stray emerged from the towel as a common domestic gray, with black stripes. He had a massive masculine head and now, as he condescended to explore the contents of the saucer, a busy tongue. They watched him drink, sit back employing his built-in napkin, and then walk toward them. He had no word of gratitude for Angie, no interest in Adam. He goosestepped silently over to Vanessa, tapped her ankle with his paw— the claws retracted—lay down, and went to sleep.

Edna came in from washing up and said, "Well, I never!"

"Never is right," Vanessa agreed. "Adam, you and Angie get that cat out of here. Incidentally, it is a male. Angie, you won't have to worry about the barn cats unless he's a fighter," she added.

Their guest opened one eye, made a brief, probably rude remark, and inched closer to Vanessa's ankle.

Adam said, "It's raining cats and dogs—appropriately. Angie, I'll drive you and your new friend home."

Edna brought a basket, removing whatever was in it. Angie leaned down to retrieve the cat, which instantly went into frenzy of bad temper; he howled, snarled, spat, threatened to bite and scratch, and Vanessa said sharply, "Let him go before he scars you for life."

Angie did so fearfully, and the cat immediately settled down, his head on Vanessa's ankle, loudly purring.

"Let him stay," Vanessa said, after a moment. "I'll figure out something in the morning."

On their way to the farm Adam said, "Well, it won't be the Humane Society; Van won't figure anything out, wanna bet?"

"No, not against a sure thing—well almost sure. I hope he persuades her to keep him. Of course, he won't replace Shadow."

"Nothing replaces what's gone," Adam said, "people, animals, trees, time. No man can walk in another's shoes —or paws. Van's lucky, really. She can't replace her youth, but her old age is just as interesting except, perhaps, to her."

He stopped at the farm and walked Angie to her door under an umbrella. "Clever of you," she said. "No one else knew it was going to rain."

"The boys in the Weather Bureau did," Adam told her, kissing her lightly. He went back to his car to head for the studio.

On the following day he stopped by Van's—he had an engagement with the older Irvingtons. "I'll tell Bing you flout his orders."

"I don't. He and Ben are justly proud of my behavior."

Adam looked at the cat. Somehow a proper basket had been found and Edna had shopped for a dish and a toy. "What have you named him?"

"Wayfarer...Tiger's too obvious."

"How about Warlock?"

"My broomsticking days are over, but don't tell Carol Benson."

"You can't call him 'way' for short," Adam argued. "What would happen if you said, 'Go 'Way'?"

"I won't have to. He knows his own mind; he'll get to know mine. Can you take him to the animal hospital for me Saturday morning? Our old vet's gone, but there's a new man there and, I think, the old assistant, Mike."

Adam complied. Wayfarer permitted transport by car and basket and Mike, who remembered Shadow, assisted the young Dr. Morgan.

The unexpected cat was well behaved; he wore an

air of resignation, and submitted to the necessary indignities.

"A healthy, if undernourished, male," said the doctor, "with a battle scar or two."

Mike said, "Remember me to your grandmother," and Dr. Morgan added, "Tell her he's about a year and a half old."

On arriving at the house, Adam made his report, and stated, "Wayfarer is out of the question; he'll never respond to it. I suggest Vagabond, Nomad, or Hobo. I looked up *traveler*. After all, I have a thesaurus. My choice is Hobo."

The cat looked up from the ball he was batting around and smiled. Adam smiled back. "I'm his godfather," he announced.

Hobo batted the ball toward Adam and Vanessa said, "I'll look after him for you, Adam."

9

In October, radiant blue and chilly despite the daytime sun that did its golden best, Carol asked Adam, "Are you still mad?"

He answered, "Of course. There's a lunatic streak in all my family," and then relented and said, "but I'm not really angry. I don't like your sneaky little ways, but I can't blame you. Besides, I'm sure Van put you in your place."

They were walking down Colonial Way. Carol looked stunning in a pale green tam and a darker coat, so Adam added magnanimously, "All is forgiven. How about dinner?"

"When?"

"Tonight will do. You may have anything on the menu, but I'll order the child's plate. I'm getting fat. Five pounds," he said sadly. "It's been a terrible summer for the body beautiful."

"You swam; you played tennis—"

110

"And a couple of unspeakable rounds of golf. It must be my metabolism. I walk a lot, but only my feet lose weight.... Let's go to the Aegean. I can't understand," he went on, "why my grandmother doesn't like Greece. She's the only person I know who doesn't. Lee Osborne would live there if he could. I had only two weeks, and fell hopelessly in love with the Islands. I used to try to persuade Gran to go to the Aegean, so did the Osbornes, but she always refused after the first try."

"I've never been anywhere," said Carol sadly, "not really. But one day I'm going around the world."

"Hurry," Adam advised. "Before long there won't be much left of it.... Tonight then. I'll call for you around seven."

At the restaurant they encountered Sam and Sara Peters, introductions were made, and Sam said, "Sara and I have decided to take an evening off," and Sara added, "Why don't you join us?"

She was interested in Carol and said, when they were seated at the table, "My grandmother liked the interview you did with her and so did I."

"It would have been better," Carol told her, "if Mrs. Allen had—well—opened up more."

"She's an oyster," Sara said smiling, "and doesn't scatter her pearls."

"I envy you the studio, Adam," Sam said. "I lived there, and Sara and I did before we found the flat. We're going to build in the spring. We own a hunk of land between here and Deeport. We did contemplate one of the houses Lee's going to build on the old prop-

111

erty, but decided to keep our stone walls and senile brook—it talks to itself constantly—and there are dogwoods and apple trees. When we can afford it, Lee will design a house—that is, Sara will design it, Lee will build it. I was apprehensive at first. Sara being steeped in the ambience of other lands, I thought she'd demand a villa, hacienda, or something exotic. By the way, Adam, you'll be our family's neighbor as long as you remain in the studio. Sara's father, my sister, and her son are considering one of the houses."

"Come again?" said Adam politely.

"You must remember. They're married, and Julie has a boy by her first husband. He used to stay with me at the studio.... How's Van?"

"Progressing. And she has a new cat." He looked at Carol who was swishing her wine in her glass. "Sorry, Carol," he said. "This must be boring, but it's all Little Oxford, past and present."

"And delightful," said Carol courteously.

"We must go see Van," Sara said. "Is she pleased about the way her book's selling?"

"What book?" Carol inquired. "I didn't know she'd written one."

"It's been out some months," Adam said, "and is about cats, naturally. Stacy Osborne did the illustrations."

Carol shook her head. "If you'd told me that," she said, "I would have had an excuse to see Mrs. Steele."

Later Adam took her home by way of the studio. "How about coffee?" he asked. "Or milk, or a glass of wine?"

She settled for wine, and said presently, "I suppose you have regiments of women in here."

"Of course, if they insist."

"Did Sam Peters mean that his sister is married to his wife's father?"

"Certainly. It's a long story and perfectly proper for the family hour," said Adam. "I never saw such a pretty nose for scandal. There's lots of it in our peaceable little town, Carol. You just don't look in the right places, though if you did, Si would unemploy you."

"Dullsville."

"Quite." He sat down beside her and put his arm around her and, because she liked it, she drew away. "No alliance," she said severely.

"Okay, but why?"

"I have logical reasons," said Carol, "and now suppose you take me home?"

On the way she broke a long silence by saying, "I'm sorry, Adam. I like you very much. There are even times when I am violently attracted to you, but I made up my mind a long time ago that business lasts longer than pleasure."

"So you're saving yourself, as the girls used to say, for Mr. Unlimited Credit?"

"If you want to put it that way."

"With or without the legal blessings?"

"Preferably with," said Carol.

Adam laughed and she asked, "What's so funny?"

"Nothing, everything, you, me, and the cockeyed world. I really had no sinister designs on you, Carol. I'm simply a pushover for auburn hair and green eyes.

Someday I'll find that painting."

"What painting?"

"The portrait my mother must have studied before I was born, only she doesn't look at portraits, and if she had, it would have been of babies' coloration. Forgive me, but I require qualities that—probably mercifully—you lack: warmth, response, affection."

"In my circumstances," Carol said, "they would be fatal."

Standing on the Westcott path she reached up and kissed him. "Thanks," she said, "for not insisting upon discovering my occasional susceptibility."

Going home Adam felt a sort of reluctant compassion for her; he wished he could send her around the world seeking her fortune, but he came out of this amused, slightly painful fantasy when he arrived at the studio. Someone was there before him, for standing in the circular drive was a brown-and-yellow car.

"Toby," he said to himself as he got out of the car. He slammed the car door and opened the door to the studio. She was sitting on the couch, with a drink in one hand and a cigarette in the other. She looked drawn, even haggard.

"Hi," she said. "Do join me."

"How did you get in?"

"You left your door open. But if you hadn't, I would have waited in the car."

Adam said, "I called you after you left here. Ginger said you were in Sun Valley."

"That's right. It's great in summer too, did you know that?" Suddenly she began to cry, silently but with her

114

face pitifully distorted. The cigarette fell to the floor, the glass shook in her thin hand.

Adam retrieved the cigarette, sat down, and put his arm around her. "What's wrong?" he asked.

"Everything. After Sun Valley I went somewhere else and I suppose I fell in love. I don't really know. I've not been accustomed to it."

"The man from Boise?"

"Ginger told you that? No.... We went off together, it doesn't matter where. I didn't know he was married. It doesn't matter how I found out. Anyway, a number of things happened; he beat me," said Toby, who had ceased to cry, "and I went home and after that to Puerto Rico with a girl I knew and while she sat around a swimming pool with the lifeguard, I had an abortion. And I've felt lousy ever since."

"Have you seen your doctor?"

"You mean my parents' doctor. Don't be stupid. I saw someone in New York—something had gone wrong. I was told that in Puerto Rico, but I wouldn't stay in the hospital. I'm having treatments now, but, I can never have children—ever."

He said inadequately, "You poor kid."

"It's been pretty expensive," she told him, "and I haven't had a job since before Sun Valley. I can get around my father to some extent. When I went to New York, I said I was looking for work and they both know, of course, that work's hard to come by. I've borrowed from other people. These treatments cost a lot. I could, I suppose, have had them for free. They're always telling you on TV where you can go for help—no questions

asked, no confidences broken. But I couldn't bring myself to do it. I thought, if you'd lend me some money...I
still share the flat with the girls and, once I get back
on my feet, I'll find something to do," said Toby slowly
sliding out of his arms, her face turning white as
ashes.

He rose, straightened the too slender body, and
thought: Ben? Bing? No, not now at any rate. He went
to the telephone and called Angie Barker.

"It's Adam," he said. "I'm in trouble—an unexpected
guest just fainted."

"Have you called Ben?"

"No. Please come. Then, if you think it necessary I
shall."

Angie was there very shortly, a bag in her hand. "Who
is she?" she asked.

"Used to live near us—Toby Markham."

Angie fetched water; she had restoratives with her.
Toby shuddered and sighed, saying, "I'm all right." She
tried to sit and collapsed.

"Has she had anything to eat?" Angie asked.

"I didn't ask her. I came home after dinner, and she
was here."

Toby sat up, her hands pushing back her long fair
hair. "I feel like hell," she said and looked at Angie.
"Friend or foe?" she asked Adam.

"A friend. She looks after my grandmother and—"

Toby giggled. "God help her! Did you tell her I've
had an abortion?"

"No."

Angie looked at Adam, her eyes twice their normal size.

"Nothing to do with me," he said hastily.

"I wasn't thinking that.... We should get Ben or his father and take her to the hospital."

"No," said Toby, suddenly wide awake, "I've been through all that. Neat operation, very successful, but it seems my chance-met friend started something besides a baby.... Adam, if you lend me whatever you can spare, I'll go home now."

Angie said, "You'll stay here. You haven't had anything to eat, have you?"

"Coffee, this morning."

"I'll carry her to my room," Adam said. "You can undress her."

"You did, last time," said Toby.

He looked away from Angie and said shortly, "Let's go."

Afterward Angie brought in a tray—soft-boiled eggs, tea, a sandwich of plain bread and butter. Toby looked at her with horror. "I'll be sick."

"I don't think so. Take it slowly.... She should have something to help her sleep," she told Adam. "I think I can get Roger to open the pharmacy if Ben will give you a prescription."

"I have sleeping pills," said Toby, "in my handbag."

After she had eaten and was asleep, Adam said, "Angie, Toby's a very old friend. I do thank you for helping. If she's not better tomorrow, I'll drive her back to her parents in Westchester or to the flat she shares

117

in the city. She has a doctor there. Her parents aren't aware of the situation."

"How old is she?"

"Old enough to know better.... No, I take that back. Statistically, she's a couple of years older than I am and, as I said, practically the girl next door, originally."

"She's been drinking, Adam. I saw the glass, also smelled it on her breath. How much?"

"I don't know. When I came home and found her here she had a drink in her hand; I don't know if it was her first or not."

"Problem," said Angie.

"More than one. I suppose I'd better take her back to New York, not to the parents' Colonial."

"What are they like?"

"Toby's parents? Rather like mine; upper-middle class, successful, square, slightly stuffy."

"I don't believe that of your people."

"Pray do. They're typical. My father swears a lot, my mother cries. They're wonderful to me, no matter how much I upset them. I'm overindulged, I suppose; and of course having inherited some money at eighteen and more at twenty-one, and standing to have a bundle— even in this era—when I'm thirty, they didn't, after I was eighteen, have the restricting financial hold most parents have over their kids."

"You know," Angie said, "you're like your grand-mother—brown, lean; you even have her eyes," she added, thinking of Vanessa's still brilliant regard.

"Throwback," he explained, "not only to Van. I be-

118

lieve there were pirates back in the line, maybe a horse thief or two."

Angie rose. She said, "If Toby doesn't sleep, if she's ill, please call Ben Irvington."

"She'll be okay. There's a guest cubbyhole. I'll sack out there, keeping an ear open. I'd rather not involve the Irvingtons, father or son. Toby belongs in town where she sometimes models or does TV commercials—and don't inquire what else. I don't. One day I predict she'll marry a man thirty years older and live happily ever after."

He put his arm around Angie's shoulder and said, "Thanks Angie, you're wonderful and gorgeous, but too tall."

"You like charm-size girls?"

"Yes, but thanks again, lamb chop," he said. "I'd drive you home, but I'm afraid to leave her alone."

She went out thinking: He'll be all right and so will his current lodger. She was sorry for Toby Markham. That probably isn't her real name, she thought in her practical fashion. In her short life Angie had seen a lot of Tobys from various backgrounds and always thought, as she did now: What a waste!

Adam watched her walk down the path, up the street, and turn the corner. He was not in the habit of allowing young women to stroll through a dark night alone. But it wasn't far and Angie, he reflected, could take care of herself. Tomorrow he'd call the office, explain that he had to go to the city on a family matter, and would be back by noon. Then he locked the doors, turned out the lights, and looked in on Toby—and found her sleeping quietly. Tomorrow, thought Adam, is another day. He went to bed with the guest-room door open and slept lightly.

In the morning, Adam heard Toby in the bedroom, and when he was dressed, she arrived in the living room in his dressing gown. "Hope you don't mind," she said cheerfully. "Sorry I was such a jerk, but when I get scared, I run."

"You can't run forever, idiot-child."

"I know.... I'm starved. Oh, not really. Coffee, juice, and toast will be all right."

He said, "As you know, you sit at the counter."

She sat there, huddled in his robe, her elbows on the counter, her chin in her hands. "I came here because I've known you most of my life. At one point, being desperate, I thought I'd beg you to marry me."

Adam, frying eggs, swore as the grease splattered over his unsteady hand. "I wouldn't marry you," he said savagely, "if you were the first or last woman on earth. Besides, you don't like me very much; you told me so the last disastrous time you were here."

"Oh, you're not my type, but I'm fond of you. Anyway, it was just an idle fancy then. So I thought: Maybe he'll give me some money."

"I cannot afford what it would take to finance you for more than a week or so. I'll do what I can. Drink the juice; here's the rest of your order. I'll take you to town as soon as you're fed and clad."

"Who was that girl last night?"

"I told you, a friend. She lives near my grandmother,

120

and since she has had nursing experience, is helpful to her."

"I suppose you told her I had an abortion and everything?"

"No. You did."

"My God," said Toby. "Right out, like that?"

"Yes. Besides, Angie isn't stupid."

"She's also smashing," Toby said, "if you like them tall, fair, and rather like a goddess. Well, thank her for me next time you see her."

"I shall. Hurry up. I'll take the train back. I have to be at the office sometime today. Go put on your clothes. I don't have much cash in the house, just eating, drinking, and gasoline money. Do you mind a check?"

"Of course not. You might mind, though, when it comes in canceled and someone else sees it."

"I bury my canceled checks in a strong box, near the little patio," he told her. "No one must ever know my true profession. Only the raccoons, if they can get through."

Toby vanished. He went to the small desk in the living room, looked critically at his checkbook and balance, shook his head, and told himself, "I'll be a little short until the next quarter." He wrote the check, put it in an envelope, and gave it to her when she emerged, saying, "Here you are, Toby. Sorry I haven't a plain brown wrapper, but it isn't drawn on a Swiss bank."

She didn't look at the check. She put it in her handbag, stood on tiptoes, and kissed him. "Too bad you won't marry me," she said. "It could solve a lot of things, for a while."

"For the short term," he agreed. "Thanks, but no thanks."

Driving her car to the city through heavy traffic and blinding sunlight he thought: I doubt I'll see her until the next time she needs help, which will be, I hope, when we're both over eighty.

That evening, after supper at The Whale and Minnow, he stopped at Vanessa's. Edna was there and so was Angie. Hobo, on the hearth, was washing his face. Seeing Adam, he ran with pleasure to cling to his ankle and endeavor, with some success, to untie his shoelaces.

"Pleasant fellow, and spirited. He's staying?" Adam asked Vanessa and she answered, "If he wants to and isn't a nuisance.... We do have field mice." A smile crinkled the corners of her remarkable eyes. "After spending all that money on him," she added, "do you think I'd send him to tangle with Angie's barn cats?... What have you been up to?"

He told her as much as was good for her to know. He said, "Stacy will be in to see you once she can conquer her spells of sorrow over the big house. After all, not even Emily's beautiful residence can afford the connubial suite—wasn't that what Lee called it when he rearranged the house for Stacy?"

"Tell her to come soon. Whom else have you seen?"

"Matt, briefly, and of course, Moxie."

"Moxie's one dog with character," Vanessa said, "Oscar's another."

"How about Charity? Well, she's outsize anyway."

Charity was the Palmers' dog, the furry guardian

122

angel of their son, Jerry. She was an enormous St. Bernard named for the heroine of a book written by Jeremy Palmer and Beth Cameron.

Thinking of the Cameron family, Adam said, "I saw Veronica across the dining room at the Pink Lantern the other day. She came in with a couple of kids to drink sodas. The Pink Lantern is a hangout for youngsters now. I never dreamed she'd be pretty. How old is she?"

"Fifteen, sixteen, I don't know; she'll never be just pretty; she'll be better than that," Vanessa said. "Have you seen Sam and Sara Peters?"

"On the run, but not for an evening since I had dinner at the apartment, which is delightful—a perfect shambles of books, prints, and records."

Angie walked him to the door, and went outside with him.

"Hey, you'll catch cold," he said.

"Farm girls don't; they just die of pneumonia, the heaves, or the pip. I notice you aren't wearing a topcoat."

"In October?" he asked aghast. "Look, I want to thank you again."

"How was Toby this morning?"

"Her usual exasperating self. I took her straight to her shared walk-up, and she promised me she'd see her doctor. I sometimes tire of being good old dog Tray. There's a dog without character."

Angie said, "Stop by whenever you can, Adam."

"What's wrong."

"Nothing that hasn't been wrong for some time. Your

123

grandmother is frail and she fights it. Better if she didn't; she wears herself out. I'm glad she has Hobo. 'Bye," she said, smiling. "I told you you were like her; you also take in strays."

❧ *10* ❧

November was the month in which Adam learned the advertising deadlines of the holiday schedules. It was a month that began with warm days, cool nights and lingering color on hills and valleys. Bushes and trees burned bright, some with leaves still green and clinging passionately to the branches. Then the winds came. The leaves scattered and all over Little Oxford there was the activity of raking. Some people, who ignored instructions, burned leaves thereby setting brush fires, to the resigned distress of the fire department.

Thanksgiving, of course, was the main event, whether one felt gratitude or not. Adam had several invitations and accepted the first, which was to the Osbornes' holiday housewarming. All their friends came, including Andrew Comstock up from Florida, with his housekeeper, Mrs. Hunt. His son and daughter-in-law brought their shepherd, Moxie, by special invitation. Emily Warner came to see what, if anything, had happened to the house where she had lived for many years; and with her came Abby Allen.

Vanessa had been asked, and Stacy had pleaded with her, "Bring Edna, bring Angie; please make the effort, Van." But Vanessa shook her head. "I have difficulty in facing more than three people at a time. Edna will look after me; she'll just go to her family's for late-afternoon dinner."

"I'll send Lee over with yours," Stacy promised. "A special plate for Hobo, and a bottle of wine for you both. Or doesn't he drink?"

"Moderately," said Van.

It was late in the evening when Adam returned to the studio. He'd had a very good time. Carol had been there, as a member of the Westcott family, and had more or less ignored him, being engrossed with a friend of Lee's, an attractive, unattached son of the area's leading contractor.

She needed, Adam reflected, an ocean to fish in, not a backwater pond.

Early the next morning the telephone rang and he reached for it, his head bemused by sleep. "Adam," said a vaguely familiar voice, "this is Victor Markham. It is very important that I see you as soon as you can get here."

"What's wrong."

"Toby..." the voice faltered. "She's ill, and it's necessary for me to talk to you."

"I'll be there as soon as possible," Adam said.

When he was dressed and had had coffee, he called his grandmother. He'd seen her before going to the

Osbornes', and knew she expected him today to tell her who was there, how Stacy had held up, and what, if anything, had happened. When Edna answered, he said, "Will you tell Gran I have to go out for a time. I don't know when I'll be back, but I'll check in then.... Is she all right?"

"She's fine," said Edna. "Ate all the dinner yesterday."

The *Beacon*, having published this week on Wednesday was closed for the weekend, and Adam took off for Westchester beset by mind-boggling speculation. He thought he'd stop off to see his parents before he remembered that they were in the Bahamas.

Arriving at the house, which was almost a duplicate of Warren Steele's, he parked the car and ran up the steps. Victor Markham opened the door. He looked much as usual, ten pounds overweight, successful, exuding self-confidence. . . . No. . .the self-confidence was not apparent this morning.

"Come in," he said. He led Adam into an impressive and orderly study, and then said, "Sit down.... Mrs. Markham isn't able to join us; she's very upset."

"Where's Toby?"

"In a private hospital in the city. I've had to pull a lot of strings to keep the whole matter—including your involvement—from the newspapers."

"Involvement," repeated Adam. "What's that supposed to mean?"

"Toby," said her father, "went out with some of her so-called friends on Monday night. There was considerable drinking and, when she returned to the apartment, she took sleeping pills. One of the girls, Ginger,

127

called the doctor Toby has been seeing. Toby left a note, not to us, but to you. Fortunately, the police were not notified. If they had been, you would have had something to explain. Read this and explain it to me."

The note in an envelope, properly addressed, and the single sheet of paper said, *Adam, I didn't thank you for the money, but I'm grateful. It has helped. I expect to get a job—thin girl advertising the rewards of noncaloric soft drinks—which is funny, if you think about it. I'll repay you, if and when I can. Love, Toby.*

Adam read it, looked up, and said, "Mr. Markham, this doesn't sound if she intended—"

Markham interrupted. "Ginger or whatever her name is told me—and these are her exact words—'Toby was stoned out of her skull. I suppose she took pills when we came home. Maybe she half woke up, thought she hadn't, and took more.'" He took a deep breath and went on. "What's this about money?" he asked.

Adam looked across the room at the portrait of someone's unforgiving ancestor and answered, "Well, she'd been having difficulties."

"We know that, Adam. Her doctor told us. We were—to put it mildly—stunned."

"Also, she wasn't working and needed money."

"She could have come to us—as usual."

"Not this time; you might have—well—forced her to tell you what had happened and about the treatments. Anyway, she arrived at my place without notice and during the evening fainted. She hadn't eaten all day. A friend who has had nurse's training came to do what she could. I promised her I'd call my physician if Toby

128

became worse. Incidentally, when I got to the studio Toby had a drink in her hand. I don't know how long she'd been there or if it was the first—"

"Exactly why did you give her the money?"

"I am not, as you put it, involved with her problems. I gave it to her because we've been friends for a lot of years."

"So she told us," Markham said heavily, "but she wouldn't tell us who was responsible for her condition. Did she tell you?"

"No.... May I go see her?"

"Perhaps later. I'll let you know."

"She needs help still, Mr. Markham," Adam said.

"I know. After she's well her mother and I plan to take her abroad."

"Psychiatric help," Adam said stubbornly.

"We heard that from the doctor, but he isn't our physician. I learned of his existence from Ginger who had called him. When Toby's out of the hospital, she'll come home and see our family doctor before we sail."

"I wish you wouldn't."

"Wouldn't what?"

"Take her away."

"Why for God's sake?"

"No, for hers. She'd be better off seeing a good psychiatrist."

"I don't believe in what your generation calls shrinks."

"I don't call them that—and failing treatment, Toby'd still be better off if she looked for work and found it."

"Nonsense," said Victor Markham.

Adam thought: Poor Toby, soon to be captive on

some luxury ship guarded by her parents as if they were the Secret Service.

He rose saying, "I'm sorry I can't be more useful, Mr. Markham. Please let me know when I can see Toby. If you prefer, I'll come here after she's home."

He drove back to Little Oxford. Mission unaccomplished.

December, deceptively mild at first, decided that the best Christmas it could manage for New England, particularly Little Oxford, was a roaring, blowing, blizzard. Everyone remembered the previous one, and, if they could get to each other's houses, discussed it. But that one had been in February.

"And before that," Katie Palmer said dreamily, during a pre-Christmas party at her house, "I fell over a great big dog." She looked at Charity who backed away and snuffled pathetically. "Not you, idiot," Katie said and her small son said, "No!" and put his arms around his furry angel. "I'm determined to finish this story," said Katie to her husband, Adam, and the other guests. "I fell over a great big dog and sprained my ankle."

"Did it hurt?" inquired young Jerry flinging himself on the floor beside the mammoth dog.

Katie's mother, Susy, visiting with her husband, Roger Baines, answered, "A broken leg couldn't have caused more commotion," she said. "I came down to take care of her."

Over the holidays the Palmers were going to Florida where Katie's mother and stepfather now lived during the winters. There was room for everyone, including

130

Nana—Cook would be on vacation—but not for Charity. Once apprised of this, Jerry decided he wasn't going, despite visions of sailboats, swimming, and oranges in the backyard. So Ross and Beth Cameron offered to take the dog. "After all," said Beth, "it's sort of my fault. If it hadn't been for an ancestor named Charity, maybe there wouldn't be a Charity in this house."

It was a pleasant group, and well accommodated in the big house. Vanessa had come for a short time with Adam and Edna. He had taken them home and returned alone. People came and went, young Veronica Cameron made friends with Charity after Jerry, reluctantly and indignantly, had been taken up to his bed.

Adam left, later pondering the possibility that Sara, Sam, and Sara's grandmother, Mrs. Allen, might have come; but only Sara and Sam had. Sara's grandmother had a cold, and stayed at home. Emily Warner came, briefly, and then returned to look after her friend. Adam would have enjoyed seeing them all together again.

Adam was busy. He went places, saw friends, worked, and sometimes contemplated writing a book.

"About what?" Carol asked, one evening while at the studio.

"Me, basically, I suppose."

"Who'd publish, let alone read it? You haven't lived long enough to be a tattletale old man. You will probably never be in politics, and haven't committed murder, arson, or robbery. You haven't lived in sin with some

131

sensational female, and your instincts are not deviant. Also, you don't seem to hate your parents, have never been kidnapped, and weren't adopted. You're not an alcoholic, and have never been on drugs, as far as I know, so if you tell all from age two, it will be double Dullsville."

"What have you been reading?"

"Thanks to the lending library, a lot of contemporary autobiographies."

"I don't mean I'd write an autobiography—time enough for that when I'm seventy-five. But it's said that a first novel is always a self-portrait because bits and pieces of the writer—opinions, prejudices, fantasies—creep in. It's just an idea. I've been a few places, which could provide backgrounds, though two days in Hong Kong might not be enough for a paragraph."

"I suppose you have a plot?"

"Only the family one, real estate plus mausoleum."

"Do you intend to use real people?"

"Of course not, although I suppose they wouldn't recognize themselves unless I mentioned the events of their lives. No, just types and sort of collages."

"Good luck. You'll need it."

"A lot of writers started on small newspapers."

"So far your genius has expressed itself only in helping locals write ads.... You'd better take me home now."

"Sure you don't want to stay—even for a couple of hours?"

"There are times when I do—almost. But there's no future in it and the one thing I am determined to have is a future."

"Barring accidents, we all have futures."

"Mine," said Carol, "has to be exciting and luxurious. I've already told Uncle Si I'm off to greener pastures come April. He's willing to pull a few strings. A friend of mine is getting a divorce. We were married at the same time and with our respective spouses became one of these suburban foursomes—bridge, the movies, Chinese or Italian dinners. She has no children and eventually is going to the city. She wants to be a model. We could team up, although the joint alimonies won't run to much more than a two-room basement. I have a little stock from my father, Hilda a little more, and we figure that once we get jobs, even before, there are fringe benefits—dinner, theater. Hilda knows a lot of people in town, couples, singles.... Now it's really time I went home."

"I can't persuade you?"

"No. I'm not about to screw up my plans with amorous complications. I assume that was in your mind?"

"Naturally."

"Sorry about that," she said, smiling. But she wasn't. She was only sorry that Adam was in her present and not her future, for in her present she could not afford even an attractive involvement. She'd gone that route before—shortly after her divorce. She hoped she'd never see the object of that brief distraction again. He was not the marrying kind and Carol was, for security's sake. She would not object, she thought, after Adam had delivered her to the Westcotts, to being the mistress of an Arabian prince.

133

Christmas arrived on the usual date. "Too early," Vanessa complained to Adam when he stopped by that morning. "Carols, decorations, everyone's jaded by the twenty-fourth. What have you there?" she inquired as Hobo twined himself about her grandson's leg.

"Presents. For you, Hobo, Edna, and also Angie. I'll come by for supper and eat leftovers."

"There'll be plenty. Stacy and Katie sent *Care* packages. Edna and I will share, around noon. She'll be with her family in the afternoon."

"Don't open things."

"I certainly shall," said Vanessa.

At two Adam went to the Osbornes'. Sam and Sara were there along with Emily Warner, Abby Allen, Sam's sister, Julie, her husband, and Julie's son. It was a buffet and there was the usual clatter of plates and tinkle of glasses. Emily Warner admired her old house and the decorations and everyone was agreeable and compatible. Emily fussed over Abby, finding the right chair and, for Abby's small feet, the correct hassock.

When Adam returned to Vanessa's she told him, "I didn't go the whole way on the food. I like snacks. Edna, Hobo, and I have opened the packages."

"Unpardonable."

He'd bought caviar and wine for Vanessa and said, "Also I've enriched you. I had Sam order me a dozen copies of your book and had them sent to a dozen people, some of whom hate cats."

"Anyone I know?"

"Toby Markham for one. She's been hospitalized, but is home now."

"What was wrong with her?"

"Boredom and temperament."

"No doubt, but what else?"

Adam shrugged. Edna, on leaving for dinner with her family, said to Adam, "The perfume's gorgeous." And to Vanessa, "I've left everything set up just as you said, but—"

"No *buts*, Adam will do the honors. Angie is coming, the Barkers had early dinner, and Hobo's eating his present."

"The best salmon," said Adam. "No caviar. He isn't as civilized or expense-oriented as Shadow was."

Angie came and they had their supper. Vanessa shared some of her caviar and wine, and Adam gave Angie a Christmas-tree pin. She stayed until it was time for Vanessa to go to bed and for Edna to return.

Adam then walked to the farm with Angie. The Barkers usually had a live tree, dug up with plenty of earth, sheathed in burlap, and replanted after the holidays—but not this year. This year the Barker boys, having come home before Christmas, had cut a tree, and Adam admired it and the ornaments, and the charming haphazard patterns they made. He brought a bottle of brandy for Angie's father, and for her mother sachets and scented soap.

He and Angie were alone before he left, in the square hall that smelled of balsam and good cooking, and Angie asked, "How's Toby?"

"Out of the hospital. I'll probably see her soon."

Angie said, "I hope she's going to be all right."

She looked about her. There was an old mirror over

135

a little table; someone—one of the girls, perhaps—had put a golden star over it and Angie said, "You make such preparations, and then...it's over." She touched the bright piece of costume jewelry on her shoulder. "But I'll have my tree year round," she said, "thanks to you."

"It's a strange season," Adam commented. "Parties, open houses, and packages, and more people in church than on any Sunday; there are even times when you forget the commercialism. Anyway, I promise I'll save up, Angie, and shower you with partridges and such between seasons—even if your tree should bear fruit."

It was then, as he smiled at her that she felt the lurch in her breast, half pleasure, half painful rebellion, and she spoke aloud in profound distress. *"Oh, no!"* she said.

"What's wrong?" asked Adam, and saw her color fade.

"Too much Christmas here and at your grandmother's," Angie said.

He put his hand on her shoulder. "You couldn't have too much of anything good, Angie; you deserve it."

He opened the door. She watched him walk out and close the door behind him. She had never felt this way about anyone. It terrified her; it was a weight, like hopeless sorrow. Her life was planned—look after her parents, work, see that the girls grew up secure and able to take care of themselves, perhaps at some time fall in love and, if all went according to the rules, marry. She wasn't in love with Dr. Wright; she'd told him so on many occasions. He was everything any woman could ask for—attractive, considerate, dedicated—and

136

she'd thought perhaps, eventually, she could fall in love with him. But Adam had come along and what happened was the last thing that she'd wanted. It was like walking under a clear, benevolent sky and being struck by lightning.

She told herself, going back into the room where her family was, "I'll get over it."

People often grew into loving. Her mother had told her that, one evening after Jack Wright had been at the farm. She had said, "I did. I knew your father a long time before I realized I wanted to be with him as long as we lived."

But other people are struck by lightning.

11

New Year's Eve in Little Oxford meant parties of various sizes and hopeful hilarity, occasional accidents, and police cars. Sensible people remained at home in their living rooms or bedrooms and watched the great surge of dauntless, noisy, waving humanity invading Times Square, as they'd done, for these many years, in fair weather or foul, and listened to Guy Lombardo popping a cork at the appropriate moment. But Vanessa remarked, "As if a change in the calendar year solves anything. The circle goes on—wars, violence, discoveries, successes, failures—people are born and people die."

She said it to Adam when, at suppertime, he came to put champagne on ice. He was going on to three parties but would leave the last before midnight.

He was doing so when Maggie Comstock, his third hostess, asked, "Are you afraid you'll turn into a pumpkin?" The Comstocks' dog, Moxie, reached up his paw and, as Adam gravely shook it, winked.

As Adam entered, Edna left to go home for a brief time to be with her parents and her young man; and, to Adam's astonishment, Angie stopped in with Dr. Wright. They'd had a late dinner at Chez Nous, gone to visit friends, and were now bound for the farm for the rest of the evening. But Angie wanted to wish Vanessa a Happy New Year.

Adam took her hand and swung it, idly. He said, "All the years will be good to you, Angie," and was startled to see her flush.

When they'd gone, Vanessa said, "Perhaps she's relenting. He's starting to look a trifle complacent.... Well, open the bottle, Adam—pour a little into Hobo's saucer, not that he'll appreciate it—and we'll drink to another year, which as far as I'm presently concerned, is nonsense."

They had their champagne and the rest of the caviar as horns blew outside and Hobo, putting his nose into his saucer, sneezed.

January was wet, wild, and white. There were storms, lulls, and more storms. The town snowplows and sanders did their best. If they hadn't, many telephones in City Hall would have rung furiously. Along the main streets the snow was pushed back against the curbstones knee-high. Unhappy shopkeepers shoveled paths, but if someone managed to cut through the piled-up snow at the curb, a car came along immediately and parked, blocking the path. You couldn't reach the pavement from the curb, so people cursed or sighed; some fell down, while others walked in the road despite the traffic, turned the corner, and, finding a small clear space, reached the pavement in triumph.

Adam walked to work in boots, and spurred by the thought that he liked walking and would shed his holiday poundage. He was considerate of his car. She was old and a trifle cranky. He protected her as best he could by driving her out of the circular driveway, parking her against the side of the house between drive and patio, and covering her with old blankets.

His social life was impaired, aside from a quick lunch with Carol or another co-worker, but he looked in on Vanessa daily and made an occasional expedition into the village to eat someone's home cooking when he tired of his own or of going to restaurants.

Midmonth Janus turned his other face. The sky was blue and cloudless, the sun warm, the wind gentle, brooks overflowed as ice melted, birds that should have been living it up in the South stayed to haunt feeders, and Stacy Osborne had her baby, a healthy vociferous girl whose name was to be Vanessa.

Toby telephoned Adam. "Could you come down here?" she asked. "We're sailing next week."

He went, apprehensively, the following evening at a time that would not interfere with the stately Markham dinner. He hadn't enjoyed his last visit. But the Markhams greeted him cordially, asking about his absent parents and his work. Toby, thinner than ever, drifted downstairs, and presently her parents left the two young people alone in the living room.

"How are things?" Adam asked, sitting beside Toby on the couch.

"Lousy. Sorry I dragged you down here; you could have said *bon voyage* on the phone. *Bon* it won't be."

"Toby, the trip could be fun."

"No. The only young people will be on their honeymoons. And I've done it all before, seen all the ports. I was in a hotel on St. Thomas once, standing at the desk, and two women came in off a cruise ship. One said to the other, 'What place is this?' When her friend told her, she said, 'But I thought we were there yesterday.' That's the way I feel. Wherever I am, it will be yesterday."

"Try thinking positively."

"I do. Have you ever figured out how many positives there are?" She shook back her long hair and looked at him unsmiling.

He said, "Well, your father welcomed me; last time he bristled with suspicion, like a porcupine with quills."

"I shouldn't have written the note about the money." She fished in a pocket. "He gave me this check to give you."

"Tell him I refused it."

"Don't make things more difficult. Just give it to charity. I could suggest a few, but I won't. My old man considers it a debt of honor, not a gift from a friend."

"Honor?"

"Mine. He's convinced that you had nothing to do with my various indelicate conditions."

Shortly thereafter, he kissed her good-bye, reminding

her to send postcards. The Markhams came to the door to shake hands and Mrs. Markham said, "This trip will do wonders for our little girl."

Driving home, Adam thought: Only a strong will kept me from throwing up.

The next evening he went to The Whale and Minnow and Pete asked, "How come you're alone?"

"I'm not. I'm working inside my head, which is peopled with very interesting characters."

"So you're writing a novel," Pete deduced, having considered this himself after dropping out of college.

"So far only in my skull. Before I came here I was talking with my grandmother, my most intelligent and sympathetic relative. But she has no use for novels. She claims if they depict life as it really is, they're too revolting to read and if they depict it as it is not, then they're instant trivia and useful only as an escape from reality. You and Jake should meet her."

"Bring her in."

"No, she doesn't go out these days. You're closed Sundays, so I'll take you to her one Sunday. Incidentally, she's had a book published, but it's about cats—the care and feeding of—with some salty comments.... How's the flat doing?"

Pete and Jake shared a small apartment on Congress Street. "It's the odd couple all over—Jake's pathologically clean, which is fine for a chef, but I like to let the chips, poker or otherwise, fall where they may."

When Vanessa Osborne was baptized, Adam insisted on taking his grandmother to the church. Vanessa contributed one of her treasures, an antique silver cup—not that her namesake appreciated it. Adam brought a porringer. Vanessa did not attend the party at the Osbornes' later, but after taking her home, Adam did. Like many young men he enjoyed small children but was afraid of infants. "Wait till you have one," said Stacy when he refused to hold the bundle that kicked and cried and made other interesting noises.

"I shall. What will you call her?"

"Nessa," she said. "Van suggested it. It sounds like something to eat and/or drink, but it will do."

It was almost Valentine's Day before Toby's postcard arrived in the studio mailbox. Adam took it into the house to read it. It was from a port not, as he recalled, on the original cruise. She'd written: *We changed ships here. We're going on to other islands, mostly French.* Then she'd drawn a heart and under it added, *Love, Toby.*

On February 14 Adam saw cardinals before dusk dropping like living red hearts from bare brown boughs, catching themselves, and soaring upward. Each day was now a minute longer. It had to be spring sometime.

Also on the fourteenth he had another valentine. It was small and plain, it depicted one heart, and it said, "I think of you." It had been mailed in Little Oxford.

No proper valentine betrays its source. Maybe young Veronica Cameron? The last time he'd seen Ronnie she'd said, "I'm still crazy about older men," and he'd answered sorrowfully, "But I'm hopelessly hooked on older women."

He asked his grandmother, "Did you send me a valentine?" and Vanessa answered, "I've never sent one in my life—but thank you, Adam, for the roses.... How's your potbellied God of Happiness doing?"

"Keeping me on an even keel, I suppose, but so far no grand winning in a lottery, and no gorgeous princess knocking on my door."

"That's not happiness? Consider income tax and capital gains, threats against your life, begging letters, and then devote a moment's contemplation to what would conceivably happen if a strange young woman appeared out of the blue—wretched disposition, tendency to headaches, inability to cook, unwillingness to clean, and —"

"Say no more, Cassandra."

So he asked Carol, walking down windy Colonial Way, "Did you send me a valentine?"

"Certainly not," she replied, "and you didn't send me one."

"I didn't want to encourage you."

March came in, bringing more wind and rain, and when the little disturbances passed, bits of the sky fell into puddles on the roads; and in sheltered places the forsythia spilled its golden libation to the sun.

Adam's parents came home, he went to see them, and a week later word of Toby's accident reached her friends and relatives. An accident, late at night; no one had seen her fall except one passenger walking alone. The ship stopped, a lifeboat was lowered, and the shaken passenger said, "She was just leaning there. I saw her slip." He'd shouted and run toward her, but she had gone.

Inevitably, people said, "Of course she'd been drinking."

She was tired of "yesterday," Adam thought unhappily.

Vanessa heard about it when her son and his wife came to see her, as they did dutifully at regular intervals. Their conversation was usually limited and Emily Steele, thinner than ever, sighed when she saw Hobo. She disliked cats. Hobo's predecessor had made her uncomfortable; he'd sit and look at her with large green eyes, as if making a judgment. This one, however, paid no attention to her and Emily said, with an effort, "I see you have a new cat."

"He just stopped by one stormy night. Actually, while he tolerates me and Edna and anyone who happens to be here, his devotion is to Adam; I'm merely a sitter for him until Adam decides to take him."

"Speaking of Adam," said Warren Steele, "I suppose he told you about Toby Markham?"

"No."

So Emily told her, ending, "I'm so sorry for her parents. Toby hadn't been well and they took her on the cruise hoping it would do her good—rest, relaxation—and then this terrible accident. Of course, Toby was always headstrong."

"Falling overboard isn't exactly being headstrong," her husband said.

Emily was drinking tea and nibbling a cookie; Warren

had a Scotch and water; Vanessa, a glass of wine, and, to Emily's annoyance, Hobo a saucer of the same. Emily felt that the excellent imported wines Warren sent his mother should not be wasted on cats.

Adam came in and his mother said, "I was telling your grandmother about Toby. You must go see the Markhams when they return."

He said shortly, "I'll write. I'd rather not see them. There's nothing I can say, nothing I can do. I saw them and Toby shortly before they went on the cruise."

"Really, Adam," said his mother, fixing him with her china blue, slightly protruding eyes, "I don't understand you. We're almost neighbors; you and Toby practically grew up together. I thought you cared about her."

"I cared," Adam said. "Let it go at that…. Edna, may I have a drink? I'll come out and make it."

He vanished and Warren said, "How's he getting on in the job?"

"So far no complaints," Vanessa said.

"The newspaper business," said Warren, "and on a small weekly at that—I'll never understand."

"I daresay you won't. But he's happy in it, and in Little Oxford."

Angie came in before they left and Warren Steele greeted her with wholehearted admiration while his mother said, "Shoo, go home. Angie and I have to withdraw." She submitted to her son's filial kiss and Emily's slight peck on the cheek, and said to Adam, "Take them out to the car…. Thanks for coming." She added, "Don't fuss over me, Warren. I'm all right. I'm just not as mobile as I once was, but trying to adjust with, as the saying goes, a little help from my friends."

When Adam returned, he sat in the living room and read a magazine. Vanessa had use for few publications, but Emily subscribed to a number for her, and Adam, glancing at this one—all sequined sex, advice, and interesting photographs—pondered on the new interest in navels. When his grandmother emerged, he said, "I thought you give these away."

"I do, to Edna. I haven't gotten around to that one yet."

"Do you ever read them, Gran?"

"Certainly. It interests me to know what the up-to-date female is wearing or not wearing, what she's eating, how she cherishes her face, copes with the alcoholics or drug addicts in her family or with the children who have gone off to live with other children. It amuses me. We've changed very little really; same problems, only now they can be discussed and solved in print."

"Angie said you're supposed to rest before supper."

Vanessa agreed to half an hour. "Stay Adam, if you don't have an engagement; finish your drink, and your education.... I told Edna I thought you would stay so she's prepared."

After supper she asked, "Was it really an accident?"

"Toby? I'm afraid not. But I don't know."

"Your mother didn't quite say that people thought she'd been drinking."

"People," said Adam, "are wonderful. I don't know, Gran...and the Markhams, if they hear rumors, will deny them. But Toby was extremely unhappy."

"It's remarkable," Vanessa said, "how many people are during their lives, yet they go on living. I don't know which takes the most courage—living or deciding not to."

When he was leaving, Hobo followed him to the door and cried a little. Walking home, Adam thought of Mary Ann Markham and grieved for the child he had known and the woman she had become. If only he had helped, but he hadn't and probably couldn't have. He thought of Mr. Markham's check that had gone to a local charity.

He thought of Toby's parents, and of what his grandmother had said when, during the evening, he had been critical of them: "It's always the parents, I suppose, beginning doubtless with your namesake and his young woman. Much of the time, it is, of course, in one way or another. I'm sure Toby's family is now suffering from guilt—which can be a very heavy burden. But parents are not always flawed or children flawless. I'm often amazed to think how your father, far from blaming me for deserting him, smothers me with luxuries, as if he were the culprit. Maybe it's a curious form of revenge." She'd added, "Unconsciously."

"He's fond of you."

"Yes, and that's the strangest part of it all. He didn't lay eyes on me until after his father died; it wasn't permitted. And recently I'm afraid I've grown rather attached to him. It can't be gratitude, and it's not a belated maternal stirring. But I'm afraid I'll never become attached to your mother."

"Oh," said Adam, "she doesn't expect it; she's terri-

148

fied of you. She's been splendid to me, despite all the tears—and she stands up for me, no matter how much she cries."

"Families!" Vanessa had said with a slight snort. "Guilt and gratitude, genes and environment, to say nothing of pomp and circumstance. I still think we should all be picked off vines, parentless. In which case, I wouldn't have encountered you.... Perhaps grandchildren are always exempt from blame."

"I'll remember that," he promised her, "when *my* grandchildren come along."

"You can't go around skipping a generation," she had reminded him.

Letting himself into the studio, he remembered that she'd added, "I think this crop of young parents are smarter than most."

As Adam opened the studio door and reached for the light switch, it was almost as though there were another presence in the room, curled up on the couch, a glass in her hand.

The light sprang on...she was not there, she never would be, and he hoped with all his heart, that there was peace for her.

12

On Saturday Adam took a train to New York and went to see Toby's friend Ginger. She'd called him. "I can't get Toby out of my head," she told him. "Holly didn't know her as well as I did. Incidentally, there are two new roommates. Holly's off to Hollywood and Valerie, whom you didn't meet, got married. A girl I met in summer theater's here now—name's Selma—and a second one is coming, hopefully next week."

He was there at two. The apartment was as he remembered it, looking as if it had been decorated by a very poor man's Andy Warhol with a touch of chimpanzee finger painting. The colors there were wild and wonderful, and Ginger's hair was more strawberry than blonde.

He'd liked her the only other time he'd met her. He couldn't remember what she did.... Modeling? She'd spoken of summer theater.

"Come in, sit down, put your feet up. Toby's things

150

aren't here, in case you remember what she contributed; her parents didn't want them, so we had a sort of tag sale—there wasn't much really: bedspread, lots of cushions, a little desk and chair. Everyone brings in something. I can't wait to see what Hortense will contribute. She's the one coming next week, a saleswoman in a very chic face-rejuvenating salon—steady job, which is more than you can say for the rest of us in this expensive walk-up hovel.... Have a drink?"

"Nope; sun's not over the yardarm."

"What happens if you decide to have one for lunch?"

"I pull down the shades."

"Adam, I didn't go to Puerto Rico with Toby, Selma did. She was over here, one night, and said she was going to audition for a night club in San Juan. Toby asked if she could go along and told us why. I hadn't a clue. I was absolutely horrified. Anyway they went. Selma's a good kid. She told Toby 'You certainly should be with someone,' and while they were there she tried to get Toby to stay longer in the hospital. Selma got the job and stayed on. Toby came home, and I got her to the doctor. He did all he could, but she was in bad shape and he had to notify her parents. It wasn't one of those anonymous clinics. Then I had to go through all that with the Markhams. But I don't know what really happened on the boat."

"Ginger, I don't either. We'll never know. Her parents have persuaded themselves it was an accident, and it could have been."

"Sometimes I think no, sometimes yes. Did you hear from her...before?"

"A postcard," he said.

"I had one too. It said, 'See you soon.'" The tears spilled down Ginger's small attractive face. "I was honestly fond of her," she told Adam.

"I was too.... Maybe your card gives us something to go on."

"I can't be sure. She always said that soon could be next week, next month, next year."

When he rose to leave, Ginger asked, "Selma might be in before four. Wouldn't you like to wait and talk to her?"

"No, Ginger," he said. "I'm sorry."

When he left, he walked and looked in shop windows and bought a small turquoise-and-silver pin for his grandmother, in a place that sold authentic American Indian jewelry. He took a taxi through the park, sat partway through a movie, and then turned up at an Indian restaurant where he was to meet a girl. She was late but flew in, dark curls bouncing. She wore a splendid pair of pink slacks and raspberry red shirt, boots, and a mink cape. Her name was Diana, but she'd once married a man named Tom and thus had become Jerry. Adam had known her since his days with the combo. She had sung with them, and rather well, for a time. He'd seen her since at intervals and they had a good, undemanding occasional relationship, satisfying and uncomplicated. Jerry had lived alone in the city since she'd left the combo. She managed well enough and had been singing in the Village up to last week, about the time Adam had called her.

"Anything going for you?" he asked, over drinks.

"Remarriage, I think," she said, regarding him gravely with narrow, slightly tilted brown eyes. "I hope you'll miss me."

"I certainly shall.... Do I know him?"

"No. It's Tom. We split before I went with the combo, which I left for—pardon the expression—a better job."

"Yes, Boston. So, you'll be Tom and Jerry again?"

"I hope not in the same way as before. Tom has finally discovered a future. When I was married to him, he was a restless odd-job man, six weeks there, two months here. Now he's in an advertising firm, copy writing. We'll live in my apartment and I'll get another job, go on working, for a while anyway.... What's been happening to you?"

"I rusticate. I live in Little Oxford, in a studio. I called you a couple of times to see if you'd like to spend a weekend with me if you weren't working, but I never got an answer."

She said after a moment, "I'm glad you didn't. I've been trying to decide about Tom for quite a while, and maybe a weekend in the country with an ex-employer wouldn't have been a good idea."

"Let me know," he said later as he left her at her door, "if you get married. If you don't, let me know that too. In either case, be happy."

He caught a local to Little Oxford. In the studio he called Edna, who reported that Vanessa was fine but had gone to bed early.

"I'll be around tomorrow," he said. "I have a present for her."

He turned up at noon, in time to share Vanessa's

lunch and when he gave her the pin, she asked, "What's this for?"

"Good conduct...You'll never earn that," he told Hobo, who had been begging beside him and now, the table cleared, sprang into his lap purring furiously.

"You look what used to be called peaked," Vanessa remarked.

"City yesterday. It's exhausting. How did I ever have the strength to work with those people? All rushing as if to a catastrophe. Everyone talking like a Tower of Babel. I had dinner with a girl who worked for a time with us in the McBurneys Point group. I've seen her since, now and then. Now I've lost her," he said sadly. "She's going to remarry her former husband."

"I trust you weren't serious about her. I can never find the right Band-Aid for the crack in someone's heart."

"Not serious; we liked each other, we got along. She was, so to speak, the occasional girl."

"Escape hatch," Vanessa suggested.

Adam grinned, "Something like that," he admitted.

April made her appearance, as usual full of surprises. After a warm and sunny entrance with crocuses polka-dotting the grass and peepers playing their silver pipes in woods and marshes, five inches of snow fell and the Little Oxfordians who had been wintering in Florida and had booked on homecoming planes listened to their children calling from New England, cancelled their flights, and tried with difficulty to book space for the next day, or the day after that. But the farmers were delighted with the "white manure." No killing frost, just the silent snow, falling straight, and wrapping tree branches and hedges in cotton wool. Nothing died; no branch broke and, when the sun shone, the snow went as quietly as it had come.

Rosie Niles came home at Easter time and asked all her friends—the Palmers, the Osbornes, all the Irvingtons, the Comstocks—to come see her the Saturday after Easter. "Bring anyone," she told them on the telephone "I'll be here through the summer, I think. I've done my job with young Rita; she's safely settled in Italy with good people to look after her."

Vanessa said when Rosie called her, "I've been put out to pasture, but Adam's here."

"Tell him to bring all his girl friends."

She told him.

"I have none," he said mournfully.

"How about your prying redhead?"

"She's going with the Westcotts. Do you think Angie would go with me?"

"Ask her."

Angie would. She said, "Ever since Mrs. Niles built that house I've wanted to see inside. But I can't stay very long, Adam."

"All you have to do is give me the signal, and we'll depart. You'll see people there you know, and a lot neither of us know, some coming from the city."

Rosie—her thick black curls dusted with more silver than Adam remembered, still thin and restless, her black eyes shining—greeted him with pleasure. You always knew with Rosie what she felt; there was nothing faked, nothing phony. "And who's this?" she asked, smiling at Angie.

"Angie Barker," Adam answered and Angie said, smiling, "You used to come to the farm and buy flowers, which—with your garden—you didn't really need."

"I like young people," Rosie said. "You don't sing do you, Angie?"

Bing, overhearing this, said to his wife, "There she goes again."

"Not a note, Mrs. Niles."

"Pity. Singing you'd look like a healthy angel," Rosie said. "But anyway, I'm too old to drag potential stars around Europe. Do come see me here."

Bing said to his son, "Rosie's beginning to show her age. Your mother doesn't."

"Everyone does a little," Ben answered, "but you just don't want to see that your wife isn't eighteen anymore."

Bing ignored that and said anxiously, "I hope Rosie's all right. I worry about her. She always looks as if she were burning up."

He spoke to her a little later, taking her aside.

She said, "I'm fine. They say no one is an ex-alcoholic, but I'll persist in believing that I am. I'm just tired, Bing."

It showed in the fine lines around her eyes and mouth, the over-thin arms and neck. But her vitality did not seem diminished. She asked, "Do you know that niece of Edie Westcott? She told me she'd been swimming here with Adam."

156

"I wouldn't know—" Bing began, but Adam, over-hearing, said, "Last summer. I called Jim first."

"She's pretty," Rosie said, looking past him at Carol who was standing with her uncle and the Osbornes. "But somehow she doesn't fit into the scenery." She laughed. "Neither did I when I was waiting on tables... nor for some time after I came back again."

Adam said, "She'll be moving on soon, I think."

"Where to? I thought she was on Si's paper."

"She is, but Si doesn't run gossip columns and she's not interested in small-town items. Incidentally, did you know I'm working for him? I bet you a Chinese dinner that she'll try to interview you."

"My life," said Rosie Niles, "is not only an open book as far as this town is concerned, but completely illus-trated. No one would be interested except newcomers."

He won his bet, for Carol, as the Westcotts were leav-ing, hurried back and said to her hostess, "I do little pieces on our more interesting residents. I wonder if you could give me half an hour?"

"Anytime," said Rosie, "but no interviews. My dear girl, I was born here and everyone knows all about me. You too, I assume."

Carol gave her a smile, half I-know-more-than-I'm-admitting, half I-don't-know-anything-at-all.

Like Vanessa, Rosie Niles had met Carols before.

Adam took Angie home early, and went back to the party. He told Rosie, "I have to report everything to Gran. I wish you'd go see her."

"I promise," Rosie said. "When do we eat Chinese?"

157

Rosie visited Vanessa within the week after telephoning to ask Edna if it would be all right to call on the day Adam was taking her to dinner.

"Why," asked Vanessa, as Rosie came into the living room, "is my grandson taking you to dinner?" Vanessa had never known Rosie well, but what she knew, she liked.

"Didn't he tell you about our bet?"

"Oh that! His green-eyed Lilith and her interviews."

"Who's she?"

"The wife Adam was supposed to have before Eve, but she left him and still haunts the night. I suppose this type of semi-rustic paradise holds no future for Mrs. Benson."

Edna brought good, strong tea and little cakes and Vanessa said, "Don't tell me you're watching your figure."

"No one else does," Rosie said sadly and Vanessa ordered, "Eat something. We can't afford to lose our star celebrity to malnutrition."

Adam arrived later to find them talking like old friends, while Hobo watched Rosie from the hearth. Kissing his grandmother's cheek, Adam ruffled Rosie's curls with his hand and said, "Come on, I'm starving."

"You," said Vanessa, "are very disrespectful."

"I enjoy it," Rosie said, and Adam asked, "Shall we bring you back whatever the specialty is at the House of Pearl?"

"Definitely not."

He had walked to Vanessa's but now he drove Rosie's

elegant car to the Chinese restaurant, which was just outside Deeport.

The House of Pearl was quiet, charming, and the food was very good, and, as Rosie liked it, spicy. "Ouch!" said Adam, trying to put out the fire with hot tea.

"Sorry about that," he added, gasping. "This must be my Oriental phase. I took a girl to an Indian restaurant the other night and thought the curry was pretty pungent, but this beats it."

"You'll cool off," Rosie told him, "with ice cream, lychee nuts, and fortune cookies.... Tell me about your friend Carol."

"No friend of mine. She's leaving our quiet backwater and going off to the city to seek her fame and fortune."

"Has she anyone in mind?"

Adam laughed. "Not yet, but she will."

"Tell me about Angie then."

"A dream girl," he said. "You know she checks on Van, every day."

"Yes, your grandmother told me."

He said, "I saw Angie frequently last summer. She's fun to be with; everyone likes her. She has a following, of course."

"Anyone special?"

"One of the doctors at the hospital. Pity she isn't my type. Otherwise I might try to persuade her to give up medicine and devote herself to literature."

"You plan to write your life story?"

"I haven't lived it yet. Shall I come around and tell

you about the fascinating novel I expect to write some-day?"

"I wish you well, Adam, but God forbid."

"You're just like Van. I can't persuade her to listen, and the only way I can sort out ideas is to talk about them."

"Try Sam Peters."

"I have. All he'd say was, 'The only way to write is to sit down at a typewriter and begin.'"

"Try Angie."

"Good grief! She wouldn't be interested."

"Her nature and her training incline her to be sympathetic. And, as she's not your type, any criticism she expresses won't disturb you. You can always dismiss the absence of accord by assuring yourself that the poor girl knows no better. I'll bet you another dinner she'll listen and even contribute.... I wonder if there's a good Polish restaurant around here; sometimes I remember my mother's cooking, fondly."

"It's a deal," Adam told her. "If I can persaude Angie to come to the studio.... Hey, what does your fortune cookie predict?"

Rosie opened it and remarked, "I should wear reading glasses, but I'm far too vain. Here, you read it."

He took the slip of paper. "Says you will soon settle down," he told.

"I wonder in what sense, physically or emotionally. What does yours say?"

"It's very un-Chinese," he reported. "It says 'You're barking up the wrong tree'—which is hound-dog philosophy."

"It could figure; I've barked up so many. You said Angie isn't your type. Who is?"

"Well—in coloring, shape, and general appearance, Carol. I've often dreamed of auburn-haired, green-eyed women, and she's the first one I ever met in the desirable flesh."

"There are others. If you like, I'll find some for you. So the outside being your dream come true, what's wrong?"

"The inside," Adam said.

"It's fortunate and unusual to arrive at such a conclusion, at your age."

They went back to Vanessa who looked with favor on the fortune cookies they'd brought with them. Edna's read: "There will be a change in your situation," at which Vanessa groaned and said, "Do train Sally before you leave me," Sally being Edna's slightly younger sister.

"Now one for Hobo," Vanessa demanded.

Hobo's read: "The hearth is the heart of the house."

"Clever, these Chinese," Vanessa said admiringly.

"How about yours, Gran?" inquired her grandson.

"I'm too old to have a future, I barely have a present," Vanessa complained; but she opened it and Adam read it to her: "You will soon meet a handsome companion."

"Good for me!" Vanessa said. "Look, Hobo's eating the pieces of the cookie."

Rosie drove herself home, and Adam walked to the studio and called Angie. She answered, saying, "I'm just about to leave for Mrs. Steele's. Are you calling from there?"

161

"No. I wanted to ask you if you have a free evening. I'd like to cook supper for you in the studio. I'm still not a gifted chef, but I can do things like steak—I can afford it this week—eggs, hamburgers, salads."

"I know," she said. "You whipped up a couple of feasts for us last summer."

"That's so.... How about tomorrow?"

"We've company coming from upstate."

"All right. Friday? I have a favor to ask."

"Friday's open. I'll help Mom with supper here, then stop by Mrs. Steele's, but—"

"Fine, I'll pick you up at the farm, go with you to Gran's, and bring you back here, all in easy stages; the Wreck is snorting like a Chinese dragon at New Year's."

Vanessa was amused by their mutual appearance. "What are you up to now?" she asked Adam.

"Angie's coming to eat at my spotless counter. May I borrow a bottle of wine? I forgot to get any."

"You want your father's offering?"

"No. I can't cook anything to go with it."

"Angie can cook," said Vanessa.

"I know, but tonight she sits quietly in the studio, her feet on a footstool, until she's called to the counter."

That evening, having supplied his guest with a glass of sherry, Adam said, "I like your dress."

"I ran it up on an old loom," she told him.

It was heavy linen, blue, and as a concession to April's temperamental temperatures, Angie had a short little sweater around her shoulders.

Adam fixed himself a drink, and said, "Everything's close to ready. You like your steaks rare? Read a book, play some music. Steak, salad, and Gran's domestic wine coming up presently."

Angie put on a recording and leafed through a book chosen at random. She wasn't reading it. She was conscious of Adam whistling his way around the little kitchen, of the spoon and fork being rattled in the salad bowl; conscious of plates and silverware being put in place, of steak broiling and the wine being opened. She didn't look at him, she bent her corn-colored fair head over the book. She had memorized every expression she'd ever seen on his face, the way he walked, the crooked grin, the sudden gravity. She wished she could stay here forever like this, for nothing ever to be finished—not supper, not the evening—just simply sitting, terrifyingly aware of his presence. And that was the point at which she laughed.

"What's funny?" Adam inquired.

"Nothing really. Me. Life. Charlie Brown."

"Well at least you're in a good frame of mind."

"I always am—or generally."

"So I've observed. But I am going to put your friendship to the ultimate test. Also your understanding."

"You're going to marry a Chinese girl you met at the House of Pearl and move to Hong Kong or Singapore."

"No. She wouldn't have me. Shall I fortify your sherry?"

"No thanks."

"We're just about ready," he said, "so I won't ask my favor until afterward. You make the coffee, Angie. Yours is better than mine."

Loving, she thought, is a disaster, at least this kind. She had known all about this kind of love, but only academically until last Christmas. Jack Wright had told her that unrequited love was plain bloody hell. And she'd let him kiss her and murmured, "You'll get over it."

He had, she thought. He'd been seen recently with one of the nurses on the fourth floor, driving on back roads, dining out....

Well, she'd get over it too, she hoped. It was unsettling—the pain, the aching, the sudden shooting stars, the black nights and then, suddenly, a blaze of sunlight.

"Dinner," Adam announced, "is served.... What are you looking all rosy and secretive about? Whatever you've been thinking of, and laughing at, is very becoming."

"Thanks."

"This way," he said, escorting her to the high stool at the counter.

"What's the favor you want?"

"It can wait. You may be more inclined to grant it after a superb meal."

"You're eloping with Carol Benson?" she suggested, smiling as a small fear bore its way into her heart.

"Me? Not with a young woman who wants to live in a city and go out every night with jolly gentlemen who are looking for a little friendly costly stimulation while visiting the big town.... Now, eat."

164

Supper over, they washed up. Angie made the coffee and they went to sit on the love seats.

"Do relax," he urged her. "I've laid a small fire, which I'll now light. I've locked the doors so you can't escape. For I am about to tell you my secret ambition, in strictest confidence."

"I should see Mrs. Steele before I go home."

"Not necessary. She's had her shot and Edna will call if anything is unusual.... Angie, no one will listen to me—not Gran, not Sam Peters. You'll have to now, you can't get away."

"As bad as that?"

"Probably...I want to write a novel. What do you think of that?"

Angie regarded him with utmost astonishment. "How could I have an opinion?" she inquired. "I mean, why? Either you'll write one or you won't."

Adam said earnestly, "I didn't mean should or shouldn't I. Gran says no, but she despises novels—current ones, anyway. Sam says no because he deals in books and has seen more flops than hits. Actually neither advised me not to. They simply wouldn't listen when I offered to tell them about it."

Angie laughed. "Try me," she said.

"You might fall asleep."

"I'm apt to if you don't get on with it."

The small fire flickered, talking to itself, and Angie listened and watched.

Adam said, "Just off the top of my head I made a few notes, but I've destroyed them. It's set upstate, on the Massachusetts border. The ruling or leading or dominant family lives in one of these stone edifices with a porte cochere and turrets. There are two guys, both in love with the same girl."

Talking, he looked very young sometimes. Now and then he said sharply, "You're not listening."

"I am."

"You're frowning."

After a while Angie said faintly, "It could be good, Adam, but it's full of holes. You don't finish anything; when you're tired of someone they just drop out of the story, leaving loose ends. And I think you're drawing from people you know."

"Doesn't every writer?"

"I don't know. I've always thought that they took bits and pieces from lots of people and made a character. Anyway, until you start to write it, nothing will be very clear."

"But just talking about it to you, I've thought of situations that hadn't occurred to me before. Thanks."

"You're welcome, and now I have to go home."

He drove her and she sat with him in the rather clammy embrace of the car's upholstery and thought: What a marvelous evening—firelight, the studio, Adam's voice. She felt her throat close and told herself, "But you cry in any situation."

When Adam had left and she was safely indoors, she went to her room and looked in the mirror. The girl in Adam's book had golden hair and eyes that shifted in color from blue-green to gray-green. She looked at her face in the mirror. There was no trace of ego in her appraisal. Adam's Doris would be hard to beat, she reflected, for she was his thought, his creation, whereas Angie was flesh and blood.

Going to bed she wondered how many women have been rivals to other women who exist only in a man's consciousness or memory. She thought of the wives of men dedicated to creating characters in their minds and transferring them to paper. Did a writer ever fall in love with his heroine?

An honest girl, Angie didn't think that if Adam's book were already published and she were reading it that she'd stick with it until the romantic end. But there'd been magical moments in the evening—being near him, having him say he wanted her opinion. She'd told him she really wasn't qualified to judge a story in the making. But lying in the big bed in her dormer room she thought: He doesn't know the first thing about love or women.

Somehow, her spirits lifted.

Adam, watching the ten-o'clock news, thought about Angie's comments on the novel, and remembered that when he'd asked her, "Were you ever in love?" she'd hesitated and then answered, "Once."

"That's not much of a record," he told her.

Now, he thought tolerantly: She doesn't know anything about men or love.

This year's summer was hot. Rosie's pool was bright with bikinis and swimming trunks of her friends whether she was at home or not. July was the worst month with little rainfall except in thunderstorms. The dusty leaves were limp on the trees. Lee Osborne

167

brought his tenant a small air conditioner. "You'll need it after a session in the office," he told him. "Maybe this summer will change Si's mind about newfangled gadgets. Edie bought one for the house—he wouldn't."

"Well, thanks," Adam said. "I'm not in the office much; mostly I'm walking or driving. I've noticed that the Palmers' St. Bernard spends daytimes in the house. Hobo is happy since my father installed a couple of units at Gran's, but she keeps the one in the bedroom turned off, the living room one on low. Says it isn't natural; that if she wanted a cold summer, she'd move where they have them, Down Under or South America. Maggie told me that when Moxie had to go to the kennels he loved it—better air-conditioning. Gran says we're going to get one hell of a storm—her exact words—before this summer's over."

"That's bad. She's almost always right."

"How's young Nessa doing?"

"So far, splendidly. Stacy keeps her naked, save for the loincloth, and indoors until it cools down outside. Once we have a spell of tolerable weather, we'll take her to see Van."

Carol Benson came back to Little Oxford early in August, bringing a man to meet her aunt and uncle. He stayed for the weekend and Edie Westcott asked some of her and Si's friends and Carol's to meet him. He was an amiable gentleman in his middle fifties, and planning to retire before sixty. He'd been twice married, there were children scattered around the globe, and he was extremely well heeled, or so the rumor went. Looking at Carol's diamond when she raised her hand, which was frequently, Adam believed it. She was very vivacious and, he thought, a little patronizing toward the guests.

"She put in her thumb," he told Vanessa, "and pulled out a plum."

"Bully for her, as one of our Presidents was wont to say, even if it doesn't last."

"You don't think it will?"

"Possibly at his age, but once you acquire the marrying habit—who knows?"

On August 31 a hurricane came barrelling up the coast. There was plenty of warning and people checked their generators, boarded-up greenhouses, worried about their trees, took in porch and patio furniture. Early that morning Adam took his grandmother and Edna to the Palmers', always a port in any storm, and then drove to the Barker farm to leave Hobo with Angie.

The Barkers had a generator, old but sturdy. They'd put it in after it was decided that it was easier to milk electrically than by hand.

It was raining and blowing. The rain poured from the house gutters and ran like brooks along streets. The trees trembled and bowed, branches snapped. The wind kept rising, sometimes screaming, as if in pain.

Angie—taking Hobo, who was indignant but composed—said, "Adam, stay here."

"I can't, doll," he said, and hugged her and Hobo to him. "I know Gran will be looked after, but I'm troubled about her. She doesn't look well."

Angie gave him a first-aid kit. "Her injection and syringe," she said. "You know about what time."

"I couldn't," he said.

"Well someone can," she assured him.

"I always come here," Van told Katie Palmer, "when we are threatened with extinction. But there aren't as many refugees as last time."

"No, the Osbornes put in a generator; there's one for all the Revolution Hill villas, so Abby Allen and Emily will be all right. We do expect Maggie and Matt Comstock. Andrew and Mrs. Hunt are on the Cape. Moxie will come, and of course, Sam and Sara."

Adam, returning, said, "Your own fault, Gran. Your only son wanted you to have the convenience installed."

"My conveniences are multiple. Two bathrooms, what is euphemistically called a powder room, and the air conditioner—all of which I dislike.... Is Angie all right?"

"The Barkers are fine, and Hobo went willingly.... Excuse me, I must find an intrepid someone with medical knowledge."

It was Jeremy Palmer who gave Vanessa her shot. Only Jeremy and Sam offered.

"Pot luck," said Katie cheerfully as the storm increased, and Jeremy went every hour to the basement to feed the generator, "and I do mean pot. Soup, salads, sandwiches, and fascinating leftovers," she said, endeavoring to restrain her small son, who was running about with his friend Charity. "When Moxie arrives," said Katie, "God knows what will happen."

"Moxie is a gentleman," said her husband, "and Charity's a lady."

170

There were beds, cots, or couches for everyone and while they slept—or tried—the storm took a turn toward the north. By morning the blow-down was over —having taken telephones, electricity, roof shingles, and a good many trees. The clean-up crews were out working long before the storm had subsided.

Adam took Vanessa home through branch-littered streets and pools of water. He said proudly, "In a pinch the old Wreck comes through hell and high water."

"I'm going to put you right to bed, Mrs. Steele," Edna told her.

"If you insist," said Vanessa and Adam looked at her with alarm. "You're sicker or something," he told her. "I've never known you to be docile."

Vanessa brightened. "If I'm ailing, it's either leprosy or black-water fever. Do stop mother-henning; it doesn't become you. Hurricanes always wear me out," she said.

"How many have you been in?"

"Half a dozen," she replied promptly.

When Adam reached the studio, he called Angie. "Stop in a couple of times today," he implored her. "I've never seen Gran look so beat and I'm off to work, late of course."

He arrived on foot at the office, wearing his high boots, and Si said, "We're still without power. The other side of the street's okay but not us.... Anyway, we won't get any new business today—if ever," he added gloomily. "I'm sending everyone home."

Adam walked down the street, stopping in at the bookshop. Jeremy and Sam hadn't come in as yet, but the others had. The Whale and Minnow was out of electricity, and Pete said, "We're closing till supper; by then, hopefully, Jake can cook. The freezer will last, God willing; I've put a blanket over it."

The worst affected in the area were the beauty shops where driers couldn't dry. The owners and assistants did everything but go up the steps of City Hall on their knees.

Everything was back in order by early afternoon and Little Oxford gave thanks. People wrote the *Beacon* in praise of the utility company and time went on its way toward Labor Day. There would be parties, speeches, and politicking, and various organizations would have picnics and balls. Adam planned to be on vacation.

Having been at the *Beacon* a year in June, he was entitled to two weeks, but it was a summer of switches. The O'Malleys' daughter had another baby, so the O'Malleys spent their holiday waiting on her, the son-in-law, and the other children. Nick Denton's respite came next, but his father was seriously ill in Oklahoma and he flew out early. Adam, mindful that last hired is first fired, could always postpone his vacation—which even in May he hadn't thought about seriously. But he was off from the Labor Day weekend on.

He paid his parents a courtesy visit and for a few days rather enjoyed being able to stay in bed, eat admirable food, go where he pleased, and then return again. During this short period he telephoned one of his oldest friends, Josh Conrad, and asked, "Can you get away for a week or ten days?"

"Sure," said Josh. "Why? What have you to offer?"

"I have an unexpected vacation and my father has offered me the use of the cabin where he used to fish and hunt up toward the Canadian border. He hasn't been there in years. A guide looks after it and Dad, for a long time, has been renting it or some years lending it to friends. How about it?"

"Why me? I haven't seen you since before you moved to the country, except that one time we got smashed in the city."

"Well, I need advice, and you're a writer."

"On the side. I moonlight. The rest of the time, as you know, I work for my old man in a humble, but paying capacity. I find I eat better."

"I thought you hated department stores."

"I do, but I'm learning to endure. I haven't taken a holiday, but I will now; the boss is so astonished to have me in the office, he'll agree.... Did you say you wanted my advice?"

"Affirmative."

"Because I'm—bear with my fantasy—a writer?"

"Yes, and also because I've known you since we were seven and trotting off to school in Westchester."

"How about this cabin—well stocked?"

"What isn't there we'll buy and split the bill. I warn you, there isn't a girl within miles, but there's a telephone if you want to go on excursions with any of the locals; there's a small village, a gas station, a drug store, a diner, and a couple of shops."

"I've had too much female companionship lately, anyway. It disturbs me."

"Why?"

"I might marry someone from sheer inertia. What else can you offer?"

"Trees, a lake, fishing—and I can cook."

"How do we get there?"

"You have a better car, mechanically speaking, than I, or we can fly and have the guide meet us; there's an airfield fifty miles away."

They flew in a small plane, although Josh warned, "I almost always get almost airsick."

But he didn't.

Josh was Adam's age, tall, heavier, with a shock of blond hair, a stubborn jaw, and blue eyes. His nose had been broken in a fight when he was sixteen. He and Adam had always liked each other and Adam thought guiltily: I should have had him up for a weekend or two—and told him so.

"I had plenty of weekends," said Josh. "Eastern end of Long Island, the Cape—those were longer—Jersey seashore. I bet you never gave me a thought."

"That's right."

"But there were girls, I daresay."

"Now and then."

"That reminds me, whatever happened to Toby Markham? I used to see her now and then at our city-type clambakes."

"You didn't know? She died, in an accident on a cruise."

Josh hadn't known; he no longer kept up with people in Westchester. "Except you," he said, "occasionally. I'm sorry. She was a very outgoing gal."

174

The guide, Harry, met them at the airport. He was half Indian, with a rugged, quiet face, and bright dark brown eyes. "Haven't seen you since you were eighteen," he said to Adam. "How's your folks?"

Adam told him, and Harry said, "Sorta wondered why no one came up this summer. Always have the staples stocked, of course, and when your pa phoned you was coming I got in other supplies including beer and a couple of fifths. Fishing's good and you'll find the cabin in order."

"It always is."

"Your pa pays on the nail," said Harry. "He expects service. The fishing tackle's in shape too. Laid in coal for the stoves and there's wood and cannel coal too. Must have been doing this for twenty years now. It's a good cabin. Any time your pa wants to sell, I got a little saved. Guiding ain't been so good these past two, three summers. But I have my traps and gun, and I make out. Wife cleaned the cabin for you and washed them checked curtains. Nice to be back up here. Don't seem like I'd known you since you was knee high."

"And taught me to fish."

"Smoke too. Your pa nearly fired me, but I told him it was just a drag on the peace pipe."

The cabin stood in a clearing, close to the lake. Across the lake, there were hills, the trees just starting to turn.

"I'd forgotten how quiet it is," Adam said.

"Not in hunting season—which ain't just now—them city fellers shooting and winging each other."

"What's that across the lake?"

"Camp for girls." Harry grinned. "Mostly teenagers with some real pretty counselors. You aiming to row across and ask for first aid?"

"Not me, but maybe Josh here. He's accident prone."

Harry's wife turned up, a small rosy woman who said she hoped everything was all right and that she'd aired the sheets and blankets.

It was a simple structure, the cabin Adam's father had bought years ago. It contained a cooking stove, a potbellied stove and a small fireplace for heat; a living room with checked curtains and rag rugs; a pump at the sink—"Artesian well," said Adam, "great water"—and, instead of the original privy, a chemical toilet. Also, a wide front porch and two small bedrooms. But the living room had three couches, two of which were made up.

Harry's wife, Liz, said, since it was their first night, she'd fix supper, and did so.

"You may not even last the week," Adam told Josh while they waited.

"Oh, but I shall. Peace, quiet, solace to the soul, balm for the wounds."

"What wounds?"

"Everybody has them. Mine are mainly caused by rejections—from editors who do not appreciate my efforts."

They were sitting on the porch, their feet on the railing. "Haven't seen a sunset like that, ever. Oh, they're spectacular in the desert and over the ocean, but this one is special."

Indoors Liz was setting the big square table for four.

176

Outside over the lake the western sky was a brilliant consuming fire, gold into red and, when the sun had vanished, the afterglow crept in, amethyst, mauve, and rose, with small pools of pale green.

Liz called them to a supper of fresh fish, fried crisp, corn bread, boiled potatoes, big soft ginger cookies, and coffee.

"Superb," said Josh.

"Everything's easier now," Liz said, "with the ready mixes."

"But not as good by a damn sight," suggested Harry. "Women are spoiled and lazy."

When Liz and Harry were about to depart in their old sturdy car, Adam said, "Nine tomorrow, Harry, if the weather holds."

Harry squinted at the horizon and promised it would for two, three days. "Okay. Nine on the dot."

Later, there would be a moon, but Adam and Josh wouldn't see it. Now the sky was sprinkled with stars and Josh said, "First breath of clean air I've drawn since the last time I was near the ocean. I'm lightheaded."

"You always were.... Shall we discuss my problems?"

"Some other time. I'm turning in."

"I have to make a phone call," Adam said. "Harry told me it takes a while since the operator sometimes goes to church or whatever. The company up here is family-owned; there are only a few like it left."

"You're calling a girl, I presume."

"Certainly. My one, only, and best."

While Josh washed up at the sink and got into pajamas, Adam finally got through to Little Oxford.

"Hello?" someone answered and he said, "Angie, how are you?"

"Fine.... Where are you calling from?"

"The cabin. I'm about to go to bed.... Is Van available?"

"We just put her to bed. Edna's gone home, her mother's down with a virus. I'm staying the night. We'll see about tomorrow, so don't worry."

"Tell Van it's top hole up here. I don't think she's ever seen the place. Cabin's stocked; we could stay a month. And we haven't touched the beer Harry brought or the more potent potables. We don't need it—the air's enough. Give Van my love. I'll call tomorrow evening, Angie."

"Who's Angie?" asked Josh drowsily.

"A good friend."

"Who's Van?"

"Believe it or not, my grandmother," Adam answered.

13

For three days they fished with some success, swam in the cool water under a warm benevolent sun, rowed, canoed—it was Adam who went overboard in the canoe —and tramped through the woods. On the fourth day there was steady light rain, fragrant with pine. That was the day they stayed indoors and talked.

Josh had a few gripes—the girl who married a professional football player, the one who followed rock stars around. "Groupie," he said, disgusted, "and old enough to know better." As for himself, he'd sold a little light verse—"They wouldn't buy my serious poetry"—and a couple of adventure yarns, but after accomplishing a book everything kept coming back, like the tides, regularly. "And you," he said, "actually want to write?"

"Well, eventually. I do have an idea for a novel—just an idea—Mind if I tell it to you?"

"Certainly, but I am your guest."

Adam talked, Josh listened and finally said, "It won't

179

do—it won't do at all. Even my ideas are better, which is to say you haven't a chance. People don't react like that, especially young women. Even good male writers fail when it comes to women. Try to understand them, and you get the bum's rush. They don't want to be understood. If men really understood women, there'd be no marriages, not even bad ones. Which is why a lot of guys I know don't bother to go formal, and a lot of gals agree with them."

"Minority," Adam argued.

"Possibly. But your lack of experience with females is so transparent that your ignorance shows through. The characters you propose to depict are as unreal as an April-fool doughnut.... Ever tried one?... Take your what's-her-name, who gets chased around the big bad boss's desk and paints herself into a corner. I doubt any red-blooded female has done that for fifty years. Blackmail's more rewarding."

"You sound like Angie."

"Angie?... Oh yes, the friend. Now I believe she really is, because only friends tell you the truth about your creative efforts. Their truth, of course, and usually you rarely speak to them again.... You honestly mean to indulge yourself?"

"Not immediately. I want to stay with the Little Oxford paper. I'd like to own it—the small-town weekly—and perhaps by the time I'm able to afford it, Si Westcott might sell. If not, there are others."

"God help us," Josh said on Friday on their way back to civilization. "Monday," he said darkly, "and the rush of buyers and exchangers."

"What in the world do you do?" asked Adam. "You haven't told me."

"Well, I'm not yet in the credit department; I don't floorwalk or manage; I don't keep a beady eye on shoplifters, of whom there are many; I'm not behind a counter. I'm just in the sacred office, the boss's only son, learning the business. Actually I'm to do a turn in every nook and cranny. Credit's coming up. Scares me, never having had any myself. So far I've just had the overview and, believe it or not, classes. I hope to wind up in the advertising department. But first, through the mill—"

"After that?"

"If I survive I should have material for a hell of a novel. I'll have had experience, which is the name everyone gives to their mistakes. I learned that in the university, from a professor who liked to quote Oscar Wilde."

"Well, Oscar must have known," Adam said.

The plane dropped several hundred feet, rose again, and Josh said, paling, "Remind me to take trains or oxcarts."

Parting from him, Adam said, "It's been fun. Call me when you're free for a weekend."

"Thanks. I enjoyed the touch of Thoreau. See you," said Josh, "and when you sit down at the infernal machine, remember, experience...."

Adam called Vanessa as soon as he reached the studio and Edna said of course he could come, and asked if he had had supper.

"It wasn't that kind of a plane."

"Then come here. Mrs. Steele said to tell you when

181

you phoned that we bought steak, hoping you'd get home in time."

He unpacked, changed his shirt and jacket and strolled over to Vanessa's. Hobo met him at the door with loud cries of welcome and Vanessa asked, "How was the holiday?"

"Walden Pond with good food, fresh air, and early bedtime. All very bad for me. I'm not used to it. You all right?"

"As right as I'll ever be. Tell me about your friend."

"One of the neglected ones," Adam said. "He's a good guy. I lost track of him—my fault, his, both, who knows? I met him in town a while back and we cased a few good pubs. Got zonked too, and we went back to his place, arm in arm, singing all the college songs we remembered except, of course, our own."

Later he told her what Josh had said about his projected book and Vanessa remarked, "He isn't entirely right, you know. Read the Brontës, Charlotte and Emily —*Jane Eyre* and *Wuthering Heights* didn't grow from experience, but from genius." She looked at him and took off her glasses. "I hate these," she said. "Inch up a little closer." Her brilliant eyes, so little dimmed, regarded him with steadfast love. "Here's Edna," she said. "I told her how to cook your steak—practically raw, the way I used to like it."

They had their supper: the filet, a big salad, wine, and fruit. Hobo sat beside Adam looking expectantly at the raised fork. Adam complied and Vanessa said, "That's right, spoil him. I think anyone who cares about you should be spoiled. They say it's cupboard love. I

182

don't think so, not always.... Turn on the radio. I digest bad news better after I've been fed."

"You didn't eat much, Gran."

"I haven't in years. You must remember I've kept my figure, such as it is, lean and angular."

The news came on, they listened, and Vanessa said, "We're going to hell in a handbasket, but then all mankind's been doing it for centuries. Just short of the fire and brimstone we'll stop, reconsider, and get on with what we're doing."

Adam said, "You failed me a while back, Gran. You didn't suggest I have genius."

"Nor have you, or it would have shown up before this like a fever in the soul. The only genius in our family was your unlamented—by me—grandfather, and his genius was for making money for which I suppose we should all be grateful. Your mother once remarked, in my hearing, that she was glad you didn't inherit my—I think she said—'vagabond nature and eccentricity,' but now and then you do exhibit a slight redeeming madness. My advice to you is to live and like it, to work, and to try to remember that you are not the sole creation of your Maker. A good many people in all so-called walks of life do believe it of themselves, and are, therefore, a pain in the posterior. Also, find time to care. My one regret is that I didn't. I was fond of a few people, I loved one, but in recent years here I've become involved with people, like Lee and Stacy and others, and of course, with you. You are really my unearned bonus, Adam."

After a moment he said, "I'm glad—and grateful."

Before he left, after Angie came in, he stooped to kiss Vanessa's cheek, and she reached up a suddenly strong arm, pulled him down to her and said, "Good night, Adam, my dear."

Bing Irvington telephoned him early the next morning and said, "Vanessa's gone, Adam. She went, as she would have wished, in her sleep."

Adam's breath was short but he managed to ask, "Alone?"

"We're always alone no matter how many are there. Edna found her when she went to take her early tea."

"I just saw Gran last night," said Adam. "Oh my God, why wasn't I there?"

"You weren't meant to be and she wouldn't have wanted it."

Now Adam had the unhappy obligation of telling his parents and Vanessa's friends, and the realization that, after the first complete unbelief had passed, he would know his first deep sorrow.

Vanessa had arranged everything. She had bought a plot in the Little Oxford cemetery, on the high hill facing east, had specified a memorial service to be attended by her friends, if they so wished. No flowers, no eulogy. Andrew had drawn up her will, and Adam was summoned to the Comstock office. Matt was there also. He and Maggie had flown back from a vacation in Canada.

"Everything goes to you," said Andrew, "the house, its contents, the little money, and you are to take care of a bequest to Edna, Van's charities, and the distribution of some of her possessions."

"She should have spent all her money," said Adam.

"Remarkable woman," Andrew said. "There's a letter for you, Adam, and one for your father. Why don't you go into Matt's office and read yours? Matt and I will, of course, take care of all the formalities."

Adam went into Matt's office. Moxie the German shepherd was there, lying by the desk; he rose, and as Adam sat down, put his beautiful head on Adam's knee. Adam stroked it and, for the first time, felt the tears in his throat and eyes, so when he opened the letter, Van's still strong handwriting was blurred.

Vanessa had written:

My dear boy, I dislike burdening you with this, but you'll have Matt and Andrew to help you. They are good friends; keep them. As for the house, live in it if you wish; if not, sell it. I want Edna to have some money. She'll marry soon and every woman needs something of her own besides a husband. I'll set down the sum, and also what I'd like you to give to charity. I'd rather you did this than have to make specific bequests in my will—which states that I'm of sound mind. That amuses me. Of all the people I know you'll be the most affected. But don't waste your emotions and energy in what is known as mourning. I've had a splendid, if unorthodox, life; I've had friends, enemies, and lovers. I've seen a great many places, and when I came to live here, I was content. Please give to our friends things you feel they'd like to have. There are books Matt and Andrew would enjoy, old china Stacy might like, and more books for the Palmers; let Jeremy select them. Also among the bequests, a sum for young Vanessa's parents to bank against whatever she wants to be, and do, when she's eighteen.

I'm leaving your father a letter also. I want him to know that I've appreciated his concern. Tell Edna and Angie each to select something from my personal junk-yard and give other things to whomever else you wish. I've no idea where I'll be when you read this, but wher-ever it is, I believe I'll be young again, useful, and car-ing. If I'm wrong, I'll not know it. Adam, I wish for you what you yourself would wish. Trust in your own judgment. I really need not tell you that I love you—I'll try to before you read this.

Well, she had, last night, Adam thought.

Later, Matt said, "She told me your letter contained instructions. What are you going to do, Adam?"

"Follow them."

"I mean with the house."

"Live in it."

"There's also a letter for your father."

"I know. I'll take it to him."

"He seemed very upset at the service."

"Yes, and my mother cried, but she always cries. Van has always felt guilty about my father. Perhaps she has told him so in the letter. In these past years he did so much for her, tried to do more. It shook her, since she'd deserted him."

"She didn't want people to return to the house." Matt

said. "She told me she didn't believe in wakes, so I suggested that after a while we—her friends—should come and sit in her living room and talk about her as we knew her, and drink to her memory. She said she'd like that."

"I agree," Adam said, his voice roughened. "After I move in, I'll give her a party."

The following week he moved his few things into the charcoal house with the red door. The house looked the same. It was hard to tell where things had been taken from, tables and whatnots. Edna had asked for the old china tea service. "I took it up to her every morning," she said. And Angie, walking around the rooms with Adam said, "I honestly don't know."

"Jewelry," he suggested. "She hadn't much, but what she had was old—she rarely wore it in these last years. There's a necklace set with cat's eyes. I think she'd like you to have it."

Matt and Andrew selected books—philosophy mainly —and Jeremy came and found treasures. "I don't like to take these," he said. "They're valuable."

"Not to me," Adam said.

Living at Vanessa's was familiar and comfortable, and if the house was haunted, as people who never knew her claimed it must be, the haunting was benevolent. Often Adam looked away from the book he was reading, or the screen he was watching, or the stereo to which he was listening—all these having moved in with him—to sense something—a presence or a thought moving into his mind, entirely detached from those which had preceded it. Whatever it was he would find

187

himself laughing aloud, or smiling, or simply feeling companioned.

Hobo spent long moments sitting and staring at the chair Vanessa had most often used, or approaching on quiet feet to lie down beside it. Cats, Adam remembered from something Vanessa had once said, are considered psychic, as are dogs.

Angie came by one evening after supper in the family car. It wasn't often that she had the use of it. The purpose of her visit was the party of Vanessa's friends on the following Saturday. Everyone had accepted—the Palmers; the Osbornes; Matt Comstock and his wife; Andrew and his housekeeper, Mrs. Hunt; both Irvingtons and their wives; the rural delivery carrier, the carpenter, the plumber, and the boy who cut the grass had also been asked. All mourned her and would come. The Westcotts, too, were asked because of what Si had said about Vanessa's letter to him at the time of his son's death. Adam debated a little over Sara and Sam Peters, but Vanessa had liked them on the few occasions they were together.

Looking at the list Angie asked, "What about Mrs. Warner and Mrs. Allen?"

"No way. Van hardly knew them. Would any of your people come besides your mother?"

"One of the girls will have to stay with my father. Mother won't remain long. She gets nervous if she's away from him even though he's doing so well."

"She's the prize guest, of course, offering to do the baking for Van's party."

"We have dahlias and asters, and late roses," Angie

said. "Mother will bring some. Everyone insists on bringing something; you'll have enough to feed an army."

"Also four-footed guests," he said. "Oscar for one, Moxie for another—the only dogs tolerated by Shadow. I may have to put Hobo in the basement."

Angie laughed, and Adam looked at her, the lamplight bright on her hair, and thought, shaken and incredulous: But she belongs here....

"What's the matter?" Angie asked.

"Nothing. Why?"

"I don't know.... You looked—well, different." She thought that not until now had she seen that particular expression and then said, "What about Edna and her young man? Luke, isn't it? Will they come with their wedding so near?"

"Of course. Edna wouldn't miss it even if she had to postpone the ceremony, which she needn't. It's not till early next month.... Speaking of young men, do you want to bring yours?"

Angie flushed slightly. "I suppose you mean Jack Wright," she answered, "though I don't know why."

"Coyness doesn't become you. I saw you two together, remember? But Van did say once that you had no intention of marrying the poor guy."

"That's right. Incidentally, Jack admired Mrs. Steele. He saw her every day in the hospital," Angie told him.

"Then bring him if he's free," Adam said. Despite the slowly dawning realization that Angie had somehow become his girl and that even though they were speaking of another man, he was not smitten with jealousy.

He hadn't had time. He smiled at her and she felt as she always did, the pleasurable pain—or was it painful pleasure?—and said, "I'd better go home now."

He went with her to the car. "She's almost as battered as mine," he remarked. "Look...about Edna's wedding...you accepted, I hope?"

"Of course."

"I did too. Suppose I take you? We can drink to her happiness and dance to her good fortune. Good night, Angie, sleep well."

If at all, she thought.

14

Vanessa's party was an enormous success and everyone said to everyone else, "She would have enjoyed it." And some said to themselves; "She *is* enjoying it."

There was food and drink, dogs and one cat, handsome men and pretty women, and the right kind of music every so often on Adam's hi-fi.

"There's no room to dance," he told his guests, "unless you want to caper out in the yard."

Some did—the younger Irvingtons, the younger Comstocks, Angie and Adam, Edna and Luke, and Dr. Wright.

It was September at its best, the daytime warmth lingering into the evening, and a little cool breeze wandering in.

Adam observed that Angie's doctor danced very well.

"What will people think," asked Angie, blushing, "when they drive by and see the backyard goings-on?"

"Just what they've always thought, if they didn't know

191

her. Here a resident witch once lived and tonight the coven is in full swing.... Have you sent Edna a present?"

"A sweater. My mother made it."

"My mother couldn't even drop a stitch," Adam said, sighing. "I gave her Vanessa's serving fork and spoon, the set she liked best."

"That reminds me, your parents didn't come."

"I asked them. My mother said it was all too fearfully morbid, and my father agreed with her; he usually does. But I think he would have liked being here." They were walking back to the house. The hi-fi was on Vanessa's back porch. Adam looked back at the yard that he had floodlighted and saw Dr. Wright dancing with Angie's young sister. "He dances up a storm," said Adam. "I didn't know doctors had time to learn to dance."

"Doctors," said Angie severely, "were once boys who went to dancing school or just picked steps up in night spots. Boys grow up to be painters, musicians, and writers, as well as physicians and surgeons."

Adam spent some time with Edie Westcott, who wouldn't dance—"My bones are beginning to creak," she explained—and during the course of the conversation he learned that her niece Carol was not particularly happy. "I guess it's the age difference," she told him.

During the first week in October, Edna and Luke were married on an early evening, and the guests returned afterward to the Collins house full of Collins siblings. There, two rooms had been cleaned for supper and dancing, and three of Luke's friends played— piano, sax, and guitar. It was very festive.

192

"All brides are beautiful, I hear," Adam remarked to Angie.

"Edna certainly is.... Where are they going to live?"

"Upstate. Luke bought a garage, and an old farmhouse—with Van's help," Edna said.

Adam drove Angie home. The moon had risen and when they stopped by the Barkers' front door, he said. "Let's walk in the orchard."

"It's damp," she said, "my shoes—"

"Do you really care?"

"No."

He took her hand in his and they walked in the orchard and saw the old elms and maples along the stone walls flaming in the silver shadows. And after a while he said, "I love you Angie. I want to live with you in Vanessa's house. I'm sure she thought we would, even though I once told her you weren't my type. I want you to go on with whatever you want to do—take the nursing courses. I'll work for Si and maybe start a better book. We'll travel, when you feel you can be away from your people. There'll be time for a lot of things, including a family. Talk to your parents, Angie, and let's not wait too long to begin our journey. I love you so much, and you, I do believe," he said, "love me."

"Since Christmas." She halted and said, "Hurricane or no hurricane, we still have fruit," reached up and took an apple from the bough and gave it to him. "To eat, together, even if it's been touched by frost," she said.

She held it up, he bent his head, but the apple fell to the ground as he kissed her.

193